FERBERT FLEMBUZZLE'S MOST EXOTIC ZOO

LEE GANGLES

DEDICATION

This book is dedicated to my wonderful wife and children who believed in me and made this a reality.

CONTENTS

THE MAPLE 1

THE GATE 14

OPENING DAY 25

GROWN-UPS..31

FLEMBUZZLED...37

FORGETTING 50

FIRST DAY...57

PRINCIPAL'S OFFICE 65

LIMOUSINE RIDE 72

SOPHIA'S ARMOR 82

THE BOOK 93

THE JUMONDO FOREST 99

THE ZOO..110

DROBWOBBLE DESERT 116

THE START OF CHANGE 131

BLORTERBLUM BEAST 136

RUMGUMHUM CANYON 150

FRIEND 158

EMPTY DRAWER 169

THE GREATEST CREATURE 173

REMEMBERING...181

THE CLOUD 189

MORE REMEMBERING...198

SMARTER AND WISER...206

LEAVING...219

JEWEL'S BABY 224

THE MAPLE

Sophia Flembuzzle threw open the door of a small house and burst out onto the porch. The seven-year-old girl was small for her age and carried an old, weathered canvas satchel, weighed down by several dense, rectangular objects. She wore jean shorts and a pink t-shirt, and her long, dirty blonde ponytail floated in the air behind her. As she ran on slender legs that were more bone than meat, she exposed the dirt-stained bottoms of her bare feet.

Sophia leapt with cat-like grace off the porch and into the grassy field behind the home, lifting the strap of the satchel over her head so it hung from her opposite shoulder. She broke into a sprint and ran across the open field toward a large maple tree.

Every few steps, she gave a nervous glance over her shoulder. When she was about halfway between the house and the tree, a tall, thin man with dark, neatly combed hair emerged from the home. He was thin and about half a head taller than the average man. He wore a short-sleeved shirt, shorts, and tennis shoes with untied shoelaces, and his eyes panned across the open field, searching for the girl.

Sophia gasped, pulled the satchel tightly against her side, and forced her legs to carry her faster.

"Hey, you little thief!" the man shouted as he began his pursuit.

When she reached the base of the maple, Sophia's lungs heaved. The man was closing in quickly; there was no time to rest.

The lowest branch was well out of Sophia's reach, but that was not a problem. She gripped the thick bark with her tiny fingers and nimble toes and climbed. She ascended the trunk with the speed and ease of a lemur, and once she reached the branches, she leapt from limb to limb like a squirrel.

Near the top, two side-by-side branches jutted out from the center of the tree. Sophia pulled herself onto one of them just as the man reached the base of the tree. She nestled her body into the joint of the limb and stretched out her legs so she was hidden from the view of the man below.

As Sophia waited, the only sounds she heard were the gentle rustling of the wind in the branches, the soft scraping of shoes sliding along bark and muffled grunts from the man climbing the tree, her heavy breathing, and the anxious beating of her heart. She pulled the satchel tight against her chest and bit her lip.

Without warning, the man's hand shot up and grabbed Sophia's calf. "Gotcha'!"

The girl screamed, and her eyes shot open. She

was now face-to-face with the man. He gave her a stern scowl, but it didn't last long; his face soon relaxed into a playful smile.

Sophia broke the silence. "What took you so long, you slow poke?" She stuck out her tongue and her lips curled upward in a teasing smile. A single dimple formed on her left cheek.

"I guess I'm not as quick as I used to be. Or," his eyes moved to the satchel in Sophia's arms. "Maybe I got a late start because I couldn't find my satchel, which appears to have grown legs."

"Dad, I think it's 'cause you're an old man." Sophia made an unsuccessful attempt at a wink.

"Me? Ferbert Flembuzzle, old? Hogwash! I'm as spritely as they come." Ferbert leaned in. "Listen, I'll let you in on the real reason for my tardiness, but only if you promise to keep it a secret." He didn't wait for a response and turned his head back and forth, pretending to be on the lookout for eavesdroppers. "The actual reason for my tardiness is because I stopped to pick this for my favorite girl."

Ferbert revealed a fresh, yellow tulip from behind his back and handed it to Sophia, who blushed as she accepted it. He then pulled himself atop the neighboring branch and relaxed as if he were in a lawn chair, the untied laces of his shoes dangling over the side.

He and Sophia had spent almost every afternoon of the last three years—even the rainy ones—perched in those branches. In fact, they spent so much time in the tree that it molded to the shapes of their bodies as it grew.

"Now, since you assumed the role as keeper of the satchel, how 'bout sharing some of the loot?" Ferbert requested. Sophia reached into the satchel to retrieve one of the rectangular objects: a book.

"This one's about birds." She read the title, "*Storks, Flamingos, and Other Long-Legged Fowl.*"

"Storks, huh? Did I ever tell you the one about

the man, the woman, and the talking stork?"

Sophia gave him a disbelieving look. "Is this gonna be another one of your lame jokes?"

"Lame jokes?" Ferbert pretended to be offended. "I've never told a lame joke in my life! This is no joke. It's a legend."

"Same thing." She rolled her eyes and grinned.

"Well, let me get on with it. A man and woman come upon a talking stork. They tell the stork they want a baby, and the stork asks, 'Do you want a boy or a girl?' They say, 'We want a girl, but not just any girl. She has to be the prettiest, smartest, most wonderful girl in the whole world.' At this, the stork shakes his head and mumbles to himself, 'No, no, no, no, no, no, no! Impossible!' The man and the woman look at the stork and ask, 'Why is it impossible?' The stork rolls his eyes and says, 'I'm afraid the prettiest, smartest, most wonderful girl was already delivered.' The man and woman demand to know who this perfect little girl was delivered to, so the stork pulls out a notebook and starts flipping through it. 'Let me see, let me see,' he says. 'Ah, here it is: the prettiest, smartest, most wonderful girl was delivered seven years ago to a Juliet and Ferbert Flembuzzle, and it looks like they named her Sophia.'"

Sophia shook her head with another blush, but then nervously asked, "Dad, can you tell me about Mom?"

She had asked this question on many occasions over the years, and Ferbert gave the same response he always did. "When the time is right."

Normally, Sophia didn't push the issue, but she was feeling bold. "What does that even mean, 'when the time is right'? I barely know anything about her besides her name. Why won't you just tell me now?"

Ferbert took a deep breath and thought for a moment. "Sophia, answers to some questions are like a tulip." He pointed to the flower he gave her moments earlier. "It starts out as a delicate flower bud with all its beauty packed into a tiny, little pod, waiting for the right time to bloom. If someone tries to open the flower bud before it's ready, they'll destroy the flower and it would never bloom into a beautiful tulip. What you want to know about your mother just isn't ready to bloom yet. When the time is right, it will."

It wasn't the answer Sophia wanted, but she knew better than to press any further. She had read hundreds of stories about children with either no parents or bad parents, and she reminded herself how lucky she was to have at least one good parent.

Anxious to change the subject, Ferbert pointed at the satchel. "What else have we got?"

Sophia pulled out another book and read the title, "*Amazing Brazilian Critters*." She smiled. "There's a chapter in here about the Brazilian three-banded armadillo. Its skin is like armor, so when it's being attacked, it rolls into an armored ball until the predator leaves. It's really cool." Sophia kept digging through the satchel. "We've also got *Geographic Greats All Around the Globe*," she announced. "I've read this one a bunch of times already. It's all about places like the Drobwobble Desert, the Jumondo Forest, and the Nocarogubby Mountains." Sophia's eyes widened with excitement as she listed the locations. "Do you think we can we go to those places some day?"

"Maybe. Where would we go first?"

"Hmm...." She thought for a moment, closing her eyes. "The Jumondo Forest. Can you imagine what it would be like to stand in a forest surrounded by hundreds of those trees?"

"I don't have to imagine," Ferbert responded.

"What? What do you mean?"

He smiled. "I went there when I was younger."

Sophia lit up. "You've seen Jumondo trees up close?" Ferbert nodded.

"Wow. I'm so jealous." She looked off toward a large hill in the distance. "I'm not positive, but I think the tree on top of the hill may be a Jumondo tree." She pointed. "It's the one on the other side of that humongous gate."

From the branches of the maple tree, Sophia and Ferbert had a perfect view of the distant hill where a narrow road zig-zagged up to a massive, metal gate that stretched high into the sky. Just beyond the gate was the enormous tree Sophia pointed to.

"It has to be a Jumondo tree. No other tree grows that tall," she explained. "But I thought Jumondo trees only grow in the Jumondo Forest."

"Normally, that's true."

"One of these days, I'd like go up there and investigate."

Ferbert gave his daughter a slightly puzzled look. "Sophia, you don't remember?"

"Remember what?"

"Seeing the tree up close?"

She shook her head. "No. What are you talking about?"

"You've been there before," he explained. "You really don't remember?"

"No. When?"

"Three years ago," Ferbert's eyebrows furrowed. "The whole town of Vedner was there."

Sophia thought for a moment. "Dad, I really don't remember."

The dark-haired man gave a quick, surprising chuckle. "Huh, you've forgotten already. I wonder if the other children have forgotten, too." Ferbert spoke aloud, but Sophia felt that he was talking to himself.

"What children?"

Ferbert shook his head. "Sorry, I was just thinking to myself."

Both sat in silence for several minutes before Sophia popped up from her relaxed position with raised eyebrows. "Dad, since I don't remember, we should go back, like, right now! Can we? Please?"

Ferbert's face sank. "I would like that very much,

but you can't—we can't. You… we're not…" he struggled to finish the sentence. Then, in a very serious tone, he continued, "We're not allowed inside the gate, anymore."

"Why not?"

He sighed gently. "Someone locked the gate three years ago, and no one's been inside since."

"Who? Why?"

"It's a sad story." Ferbert shook his head. "There's no sense in spoiling a beautiful day like today with a sad story. Which book do you want?"

"I don't know. I guess I'll take *Geographic Greats*."

"Great. I'll take the one about Brazilian critters."

Sophia opened her book and started reading, but she found it difficult to focus. She wanted answers. She wanted to know what her dad wasn't telling her. She wanted to remember whatever it was that she had forgotten, and she didn't understand why her dad wouldn't talk about it.

Ferbert also struggled to focus on his book. He

was thinking about what he hadn't told Sophia. He was thinking about the gate on the hill and about the day a salesman named Gus Gates knocked on his door more than three years earlier.

THE GATE

Over three years earlier, a man knocked on the front door of Ferbert's small home.

"I'm Gus Gates of Gus's Gates, the greatest gates on the globe, and I'm here to sell you a gate." The man was wearing a neatly-pressed suit and a polka-dot bow tie. "I can get you any kind of gate, and my gates are guaranteed. I've got gorgeous gates, grand gates, glamorous gates, and gargantuan gates. I've got gates that glitter and glimmer and gates that glisten and glow. I've got gates that are grouchy, gleeful, gutsy, and groovy! I've got gates that giggle, gates that growl, gates that grow, and gates that groan. From boring, old galvanized to glorious and golden, Gus's Gates are guaranteed to be gamble-free." The man studied Ferbert's reaction after finishing his pitch.

"I'm quite sorry, Mr. Gates," Ferbert began, "but I have no need for a gate."

"Oh?" An amused smile widened across Mr. Gates' face. "I greatly doubt that. I have good reason to guesstimate you have great need for a gate."

"How do you figure?"

The man straightened his suit coat, leaned forward, and waved for Ferbert to do so, as well. Then, in frank, sincere language, Mr. Gates whispered, "I think you will be very interested to know that your house is not on my normal sales route. In fact, I would never have come this way—not in a hundred years—but you see…" Mr. Gates hesitated before continuing, "I was led here by the most curious of things: a cloud, if you can believe that." He pointed to the sky above them, and Ferbert's gaze followed.

When he saw the cloud to which Mr. Gates was referring, his eyes widened and his neck hairs tingled. His complete and undivided attention was on the man with the bow tie. "Alright, I'm listening. Just what kind of gate do you think I need?"

"Ahhh." Mr. Gates winked and went back to using his normal salesman voice. "I think you need a gate so grand it can be seen from miles away—a gate that stands as an invitation to something great. Yes, I will get you a gate that gathers. People will wait in lines a mile long just to see what's on the other side." Mr. Gates touched the tip of his nose and asked, "Would a gate like that do the trick?"

Ferbert looked up toward the cloud again. "It seems you know exactly what I need."

"Very well. I'll make a gate so grand you will need ten of the tallest ladders just to reach the top. Naturally, it will come with a key so grand only a giant could fit it in his pocket. Mark my words, when the day comes to open the gate, men, women, and children will line up as far as the eye can see to see what is on the other side."

When the gate was installed, Ferbert, true to the word of Mr. Gates, had to use ten of the tallest ladders to reach the top. Above the gate, he hung a sign that read:

FLEMBUZZLE ZOO:
THE MOST EXOTIC ZOO IN THE
WORLD

Beneath the sign, he hung a banner with the words "Opening Next Spring."

Rumors about Flembuzzle Zoo reached nearly every corner of the neighboring town of Vedner before the sun set. There had never been a zoo in Vedner, so the rumors were charged with excitement.

Fathers bragged at work that they would be the first in line the day it opened. Mothers made plans to forever abandon the parks they typically visited and spend every day at the new zoo. Children spent their entire school recess imitating the most exotic creatures they could think of.

Max Monev, the mayor of Vedner, was less than thrilled when he first learned about the zoo, but he soon hatched a plan that gave him reason to be eager for the zoo's grand opening.

The plan was hatched the day that his assistant, Derek Dunger, had asked, "Sir, have you heard about this Flembuzzle Zoo that everyone in town is talking about?"

"What do you mean everyone's talking about it? What are they saying?" Mayor Monev had responded.

"They say it's going to be the greatest thing to ever happen in Vedner."

"Nonsense—I'm the greatest thing that has ever happened to Vedner! Surely people are still talking about how great I am. Are they not?"

"Sir, all I've been hearing for days now is talk of Flembuzzle Zoo. Not one mention of you."

Mayor Monev gritted his teeth, "Who is this Flembuzzle character and who does he think he is?"

"No one knows, sir. There are rumors that a few citizens saw him put up the sign, but no one knows anything about him."

"You mean to tell me that a stranger made my people forget about me, their greatest mayor, all because he put up a silly gate that happens to be really big."

"Sir, I doubt they have forgotten you. Who could forget you? They just aren't talking about you at the moment."

"A moment is too long. Perhaps we should knock the gate down and tell everyone to forget about it."

"I don't think that would be a good idea. People

are really excited about this zoo; I worry that knocking down the gate may make you very unpopular."

"I don't suppose you have a better idea?"

"There is that saying, 'If you can't beat them, join them.'"

"Dunger, you're clever, but I'm wise," Mayor Monev grinned. "I'll do better than joining—I'll take credit!"

That very day, Mayor Monev called a town meeting and put his plan to work.

"People of Vedner, I have been working for a very long time on what I was hoping would be a big surprise, but I understand rumors are already floating around, and I wanted to make sure you all knew the full truth." Mayor Monev spoke with the passion of someone that actually believed his own lies. "It is true that Vedner will soon be home to the most exotic zoo in the world, but what you may not know is that I, your humble mayor, am the one that made it all happen."

The citizens erupted in applause, and someone yelled, "Three cheers for Mayor Monev! Hip hip, hooray! Hip hip, hooray! Hip hip, hooray!"

Mayor Monev was a natural at taking undeserved credit, but he was also a natural at getting carried away and saying things he regretted. This was especially true when people cheered for him. Hungry for more applause, he said what would become his greatest regret. "When Flembuzzle Zoo opens, people will flock to Vedner and we will be ready. Businessmen must build more businesses; shopkeepers need more shops; home builders must build more homes; and road pavers must pave more roads. We need more hotels, restaurants, school houses, and farms. Build them all!"

Over the next year, the people of Vedner did just as he said. The town doubled, tripled, and then quadrupled in size.

On the eve of the opening of Flembuzzle Zoo, the citizens gathered in Town Square to celebrate with a parade, rides, games, shows, popcorn, and cotton candy. The night ended with the largest fireworks show the town of Vedner had ever put on, but just before it began, Mayor Monev stood atop of the steps to Town Hall.

He was a man of odd proportions: tall with a thick neck, broad shoulders, strong arms, a round but solid belly, and long, chicken legs. His hair was slick and well-manicured with each strand in its place. For anyone else, his extravagant suit would have been overdressing for the occasion, but this lofty apparel was typical for Mayor Monev.

He boomed into the microphone, "People of Vedner, tomorrow is the opening of Flembuzzle Zoo: The Most Exotic Zoo in the World, and tonight we celebrate how my leadership is about to change this town forever." The people cheered, whistled and clapped, and Mayor Monev soaked it up before continuing. "Now, before we kick off the fireworks, I think it would only be appropriate to honor Mr. Flembuzzle by letting him come up here for a photo with the marvelous Mayor Max Monev. Come on up, Mr. Flembuzzle!"

Citizens cheered louder and longer than before, but when the whistling died down and the clapping slowed to a stop, Ferbert Flembuzzle was nowhere to be seen.

Mayor Monev spoke in to the microphone again with a clear tone of confusion and embarrassment. "Mr. Flembuzzle? You don't want to miss this once-in–a-lifetime opportunity to stand shoulder-to-shoulder with your great mayor." Mayor Monev covered the microphone, leaned over to Dunger and whispered, "Where is that man, Flembuzzle? I look like a fool."

"I don't know, sir," Dunger responded. "Did anyone invite him?"

"Invite him?" the mayor questioned through

clenched teeth. "Everyone in town has been talking about this day for a year now—an invitation hardly seemed necessary."

Dunger shrugged. Mayor Monev turned his charisma back on and spoke into the microphone again. "I've just been informed that Mr. Flembuzzle is not here because he is preparing for our arrival tomorrow morning, but he sends his regrets and wanted you to know how grateful he is for all my hard work," he lied. "Let the fireworks begin!"

No one had invited Ferbert to the celebration, and no one had told him it was in honor of his zoo. In fact, no one in Vedner had ever met or spoken to Ferbert. What they and especially the mayor didn't know, was what to expect when the gate to Flembuzzle Zoo opened.

OPENING DAY

The morning after the celebration in Town Square, Flembuzzle Zoo was scheduled to open. The entire town of Vedner was radiating with excitement. Hours before it opened, families started lining up on the mile-long zig-zag road leading to the gate.

When Ferbert arrived, the line already extended to the bottom of the hill. He politely pressed through the crowd with his arms wrapped around the giant key. He was nervous—so nervous that he accidently tripped over his untied shoelaces, tumbled forward, and crashed into a large man.

"Hey!" the man yelled as he turned around to face Ferbert. "Watch where you're going, you big—" He froze midsentence when he saw the large key in Ferbert's arms and looked to the giant gate realizing he was standing face to face with Mr. Flembuzzle.

"I'm quite sorry," Ferbert began. "I must have tripped over my laces and I—"

"No, no, no," the man apologized. "I am the one who's sorry. Please forgive me. Had I known I was talking to the man who built this zoo, I wouldn't have snapped."

The man's statement drew the attention of the crowd around him, and whispers spread up the line.

"Is it really him?"

"Who else would have the key to the gate?"

"Hurry, everyone, out of his way!"

The crowd parted and created a clear path.

"Now, now," the large man said as he dusted off Ferbert's shoulders. "Everyone's waiting on you. Don't let me keep you any longer."

"Thank you, sir."

Before Ferbert could take two steps, however, the man yelled out again, "Wait! Your shoelaces—let me tie 'em for ya." The man started to bend down.

"No, please leave them just as they are," Ferbert responded without pause. "I never tie them."

The man stepped back and scratched his head, unsure how to respond, and Ferbert continued up the road followed by a small girl no one seemed to notice. When he neared the top of the hill and emerged from the crowd, he saw Mayor Monev at the front of the line surrounded by newscasters and photographers.

When the mayor saw a man with an enormous key in his arms, he whispered to Derek Dunger, "This must be the fella we've been waiting for." Mayor Monev marched directly toward Ferbert, and the newscasters and photographers followed with flashing cameras. "Mr. Flembuzzle," the mayor spoke with the tone of someone greeting an old friend, though he still wasn't entirely sure he was greeting the right person.

"Yes, I'm Ferbert Flembuzzle," he responded as he shook the mayor's now outstretched hand. "Welcome to my zoo, Mr...."

"I'm Mayor Max Monev. It is a pleasure and honor to have your zoo here in Vedner." As he spoke, he gave Ferbert's hand a vigorous shake, then turned toward the newscasters and photographers with a broad, well-rehearsed smile. From the corner of his mouth, he whispered, "Smile big, Mr. Flembuzzle. This is the biggest day in the history of Vedner, and you have the pleasure of being photographed with the most important man in town."

The men stood and smiled for flash after flash of the cameras with Mayor Monev wearing a broad, flashy grin to match his extravagant suit. His arm wrapped around Ferbert, with his long, ugly, crooked fingers curling around the shoulder.

After several moments, a newsman threw a microphone in Ferbert's face and asked, "Mr. Flembuzzle, can you tell us what exotic animals we'll have the pleasure of seeing today? Do you have any white tigers? Panthers?"

"White tigers?" he questioned with confusion. "Anyone can see a white tiger. The animals in my zoo are nothing like that."

The newsman, upon hearing this, turned toward the camera. "Ladies and gentlemen, you heard it straight from the mouth of Mr. Flembuzzle: the exotic white tiger is not exotic enough for Flembuzzle Zoo. This day is going to be more spectacular than Vedner could have ever imagined."

Mayor Monev, starving to have the spotlight back on him, slapped Ferbert's back. "Enough talk; let's open the gate, already!"

The crowd fell silent as Ferbert approached the gate with the giant key in hand. He took a deep breath as he pressed it into the keyhole, and as he turned the key, he wondered if the people of Vedner were ready for his zoo. A crisp click sang through the air and Ferbert pushed open both sides of the enormous gate.

"Flembuzzle Zoo is now open for business," he announced, with a slight crack in his voice, as he took a seat behind the ticket counter.

The crowd erupted in cheers and rushed in behind Mayor Monev, throwing handfuls of cash at Ferbert without waiting for change. In a matter of minutes, every citizen of Vedner was through the gate.

GROWN-UPS

As soon as there was no one left outside the gate, Ferbert and the small girl at his side ventured into the zoo. As he pressed his way through the crowds, he noticed the people looked confused. Farther in, they appeared disappointed. Farther still, they were angry and outraged.

"Oh no!" he gasped, his heart sinking. "No, no, no! They don't see!"

Ferbert ran to the giant Jumondo bird exhibit and discovered people packed around the short fence encircling the exhibit, in the middle of which was an enormous, towering Jumondo tree.

"Where is it?" someone asked.

"Maybe it's in the high branches, too high to be seen," another person suggested.

"That can't be," someone else replied. "The sign says the giant Jumondo bird is the largest bird in the world. We should be able to see it even in the highest branches."

"Wait, I see branches moving!"

"It's just the wind."

"I don't see any birds, and I certainly don't see the largest bird in the world."

"Maybe it escaped. After all, there's just a short barrier—the thing probably flew away."

"Maybe it's one of those birds that doesn't fly."

A small, freckle faced girl suddenly yelled out, "I see it! It's right there. It's amazing!"

"Where? I still don't see it," someone responded.

"Right there. It's right there!" the child called out, pointing toward the Jumondo tree, her strawberry blonde hair bouncing as she jumped with excitement.

The girl's father knelt down to be at eye level. "Sweetie, what does it look like? Is it in the tree? Is it behind the tree? Where do you see it?"

Her lips tightened with frustration. "Dad, it's right there." She pointed toward the tree again.

The dad tried to hide his humiliation by forcing a smile and whispered to his daughter, "Sweetie, I think you misheard me. The sign says there's supposed to be a Jumondo bird, not a Jumondo tree." He then stood and apologized to the crowd. "My daughter is just a little confused. She didn't see anything."

As he made this announcement, the girl's joy faded away; her jumping stopped and the smile disappeared from her lips. She felt certain she had seen the giant Jumondo bird, but now she only felt embarrassed. The girl glanced back toward the exhibit for one final look and happened to see

Ferbert Flembuzzle standing on the other side.

Ferbert, having watched the whole thing, was smiling at the girl. The smile was soft and genuine and seemed to say, "You saw it, and these grown-ups can't take that away from you, unless you let them."

The freckle faced girl smiled back as her father grabbed her by the hand and pulled her away, grumbling under his breath.

Ferbert then hurried to the Drobwobble tortoise exhibit, which consisted of a large, sand-covered oasis with a large pond surrounded by several tall palm trees. To Ferbert's dismay, the reactions he found there were similar.

Amongst the mumbles and grumbles of the crowd, a young boy with shorn black hair pointed to the pool of water and told the grown-ups he saw the tortoise. His mother studied the exhibit for some time before shaking her head and giving her son a look that suggested she was ashamed of what he had said.

"I don't know what you think you're seeing, but there's clearly something wrong with your eyesight. I am taking you to the eye doctor as soon as we leave."

The boy's enthusiasm deflated as his mother dragged the boy right past Ferbert, who displayed the same smile he'd given the girl. The boy, regaining his confidence smiled back as his mother whisked him away.

At the Blorterblum bush beast exhibit, a mother scolded her daughter for announcing that she saw the amazing creature. "Get a hold of your imagination and stop pretending you can see animals."

The daughter was devastated, but as tears began to well up, she caught sight of Ferbert's comforting smile and stopped crying.

Similar scenarios played out at every exhibit he visited. Parents rebuked their children for seeing creatures, and child after child caught sight of Ferbert's smile, reassuring them that they had seen something fantastic.

FLEMBUZZLED

Mayor Monev had pressed his way through the entire zoo ahead of everyone else and had spent no more than a minute or two at each exhibit, starting with the giant Jumondo bird.

"Nothing," he'd mumbled to himself while standing in the shade of the massive Jumondo tree. He marched to the next exhibit. "Nothing here, either."

Mr. Dunger was at the mayor's heels each step of the way, voicing his agreement at every chance. "Indeed, sir. Good eye. Nothing to see in the least."

At the third exhibit—and every exhibit after that—Mayor Monev simply groaned from his throat like a toad and said nothing. When he'd seen every exhibit, the mayor's face was red with anger and then pale with worry.

"We've been swindled," he grumbled before collapsing onto a bench and dropping his face into his hands. "No one will come from anywhere to see this place."

"Agreed," Dunger had responded.

"I doubled the size of this town two times over because this zoo was supposed to bring people here! I told the people this zoo was my doing! I'm ruined."

"Sir, perhaps we should slip out before anyone confronts us?" Dunger suggested.

"Quite right."

The two started weaseling their way toward the gate but didn't make it ten feet before a businessman jumped into their path.

"You promised us people from all over would

come to Vedner because of the exotic creatures in this zoo, but there aren't any animals!" the man yelled. "What are we supposed to do with our new businesses?"

One by one, people began crowding around Mayor Monev and broadcasting their complaints.

"Who's going to shop at our new shops?"

"Who's going to live in our new homes?"

"Who's going to drive on our new roads?"

"Who's going to stay in our new hotels?"

"Who's going to eat at our new restaurants?"

"Who will attend our new schools?"

"Who will eat the food grown on our new farms?"

There was no escape—nowhere to run or hide. Cornered by angry faces, Mayor Monev had stood on a bench and did the two things he did best: gave a speech and mixed truths with lies.

"People of Vedner, this is a horrible day for everyone. The whole town has worked hard for this day, and you deserve to be rewarded for your hard work. Unfortunately, it looks like that won't happen. You elected me to be your mayor, though, because I am a leader who can fix problems."

The words flowed off the mayor's tongue with ease as he simultaneously plotted out how to redirect the people's anger away from him. As he spoke, he caught sight of Ferbert at the back of the crowd. An idea formed in the mayor's rotten brain.

"Before I work to fix your problems," Mayor Monev continued, "you should ask yourself: whose fault is this? Who deserves the blame for all our problems? Who could bear to do something so awful to each of you?" In a dramatic show, he paused, put both hands over his heart and softened his eyes.

"Would someone who loves Vedner cause your problems? No. The person to blame doesn't love Vedner the way I do. He's a conman, a trickster, and an outsider, and I am sorry to say that, even me, your humble and trusting Mayor Max Monev, fell prey to the con." He stared directly at Ferbert as he continued, "Look around you. Do you see the outsider?" The people began looking from side to side and casting suspicious glares at one another. "I see the outsider right there!" He snapped his arm out, his long, ugly finger stabbing through the air, and everyone turned. "Ferbert Flembuzzle is to blame!"

Mayor Monev let this accusation sink in for a moment; when he continued, he shifted his tone to speak to the townspeople in the same way a loving parent breaks bad news to their children.

"Mr. Flembuzzle knew we were a trusting people, and what did he do with that trust? He promised us a zoo, but not any old zoo—the most exotic zoo in the whole world, so amazing that the town of Vedner would quadruple in size. Being the good people we are, we trusted him and spent nearly everything making the town bigger. Then, he took the last of our money as we came through that gate with the promise of seeing exotic animals. Well, I looked everywhere and there isn't a single animal in this so-called zoo. Mr. Flembuzzle lied to all of us." Mayor Monev shook his head in disgust.

Ferbert spoke in a calm voice. "This *is* the most exotic zoo in the world. It's right in front of you! You will see it, but you have to open your eyes and believe."

"It's true!" the freckle faced boy called out. "I saw them."

"I saw them, too!" the boy from the Drobwobble tortoise exhibit exclaimed.

"Me too!" another child had blurted out, followed by another. Child after child joined the throng of voices defending Ferbert.

Mayor Monev exploded in a trumpeting roar, "This is precisely the trickery I am talking about! Not only has Mr. Flembuzzle lied to us, but look at what he has also done to your sweet, beautiful, innocent children. He's poisoned their minds and made them think they are seeing things that don't exist! Now, with his pockets stuffed full of your money, he has the nerve to claim something is wrong with our eyes." The mayor looked at Ferbert, puffed up his chest and narrowed his eyes to signal that he would not stand down. "There's nothing to believe. We've all been lied to—tricked. We've all been… Flembuzzled!"

Everyone in the zoo burst out in an uproar of complaint, demanding both their money back and that Ferbert be punished for *Flembuzzling* the whole town. Mayor Monev threw his hands in the air and waved them downward, motioning for the crowd to calm themselves.

"Good people of Vedner, I will fix this and make sure Mr. Flembuzzle doesn't get away with what he has done." Mayor Monev leapt off the bench and cut through the crowd toward Ferbert. When he reached him, he pressed his ugly finger against

Ferbert's chest. "I order you to pay back every dollar you collected and apologize to these good people right here and now, and I forbid you from calling this place a zoo ever again!"

Ferbert stood in calm silence for a brief moment before turning to the angry crowd. "I wish you could see it—what your children and I see—but I understand it may take some time. I couldn't see it at first, either, so I will give you time." He turned back to Mayor Monev and, in a voice that was both gentle and firm, explained, "If necessary, I'll stay until I die and my daughter inherits the zoo."

"Your daughter?" Mayor Monev exclaimed. "What daughter?"

The four-year-old girl that had been at Ferbert's side all morning stepped out from behind Ferbert's legs. For the first time, the people of Vedner took notice of her. "This is my daughter, Sophia," he explained. Sophia gave an enchanting smile, triggering contagious whispers.

"He has a daughter?"

"He's a father?"

"Surely he wouldn't lie to his own child."

"Is it possible our children really did see something?"

As the whispers spread, Mayor Monev felt trembling anger swell within him, starting at his heart and growing to the tips of his fingers and tongue.

He erupted in a booming yell that silenced all the whispers, "That is quite enough of your games and lies, Mr. Flembuzzle! Before you came here, Vedner was a calm and peaceful town, but your lies have ruined us. I will not allow you to Flembuzzle the good people of Vedner like you Flembuzzled our children, and I want you out of here! I want you gone, now!"

Mr. Dunger leaned forward and whispered in Mayor Monev's ear, "Sir, are you sure you want to send him away?"

"Why wouldn't I?" the mayor whispered back in an irritated tone.

"Well, sir, you have done an excellent job making these people forget all the credit you took and shifting the blame to this man, and I think we want to keep it that way, don't we?"

"What's your point, Dunger?" Mayor Monev struggled to maintain a whisper.

"Sir, every time these people look at their empty businesses, homes, schools, and roads, they will be reminded of this day and they will be angry. Today, they are angry with Flembuzzle, but the question is, who will they be angry with tomorrow? If Flembuzzle stays, we can make sure the anger stays directed toward him and his pipsqueak daughter."

"Dunger, once again you prove to be a clever man."

Mayor Monev turned back to the crowd and resumed his booming voice. "Yes, Mr. Flembuzzle, I want you gone, but... a good leader must be both forgiving and compassionate, and I am both, so I have decided you can stay. There will be terms, though. First, you have only until your daughter's eighth birthday to show these level-headed citizens what you claim is here. If we don't see it, I will drive you out like the filthy rat you are."

"Very well," Ferbert responded. "I trust that, as parents return here with their children, they will one day see what I, my daughter, and your children see."

The mayor burst out with a cruel laugh before continuing, "That brings me to my second term: the gate will remain locked. I can't have you robbing my people anymore, or casting spells on the children." Mayor Monev yanked the giant key out of Ferbert's hands and, in a conniving whisper, added, "Good luck convincing anyone to believe you when not even you will be able to get through the gate."

He then stood tall and announced to everyone, "From this day forward, no one is allowed to enter this z—" the mayor caught himself. "This… this…

whatever it is!" The mayor turned and started to walk out. Then he paused and turned back. "And Mr. Flembuzzle, when I say no one, I mean no one." He lifted his long, ugly finger and pointed at Sophia. "That includes you and her." With that, he turned around and stormed out of the zoo, followed by the people of Vedner.

When the last person had exited, the mayor locked the gate with the giant key and then drove off in his limousine. A few minutes later, two workers arrived—one with ten ladders and another with a new, smaller sign. The first climbed to the top of the ladders, where he removed the bolts from Ferbert's sign. It fell to the ground and splintered into a hundred pieces. The other worker hung the new sign at the bottom of the gate. It read:

THIS IS NOT A ZOO.
NO ONE ALLOWED INSIDE.

"What just happened?" Sophia asked her dad in a soft voice. "What does it say?"

Ferbert looked down at his daughter with tears in his eyes. "It says we can't go inside anymore."

FORGETTING

From that moment forward, the grown-ups in Vedner began using the term *Flembuzzled* every day as a curse and byword. At first, they'd said it only to describe being tricked by someone else, but it didn't take long before the term was used to describe every unpleasant event or unfortunate circumstance.

If someone lost their car keys or had to wait in a long line, they insisted they were being Flembuzzled. When the weather was unpleasant or teenagers had been caught doing something wrong, they complained of being Flembuzzled.

In every speech Mayor Monev gave, he told the grown-ups that the one thing they must never forget was how Ferbert Flembuzzle had Flembuzzled them all. Every speech ended with this warning: "Above all else, never trust a Flembuzzle."

The only people who didn't use the term were the children who'd seen the creatures in Ferbert's zoo. That, however, did not last forever. As the months went by, the children's memories faded. They forgot about what they had seen at the zoo, including Ferbert's smile. In time, even the small children told tales of being Flembuzzled when things didn't go their way.

All of this was unknown to Sophia, who was never taken into town during the three years following the closure of the zoo. Instead, Sophia spent her days at home, outside of town. In the days immediately following the gate being locked, Sophia talked about the zoo often and frequently begged Ferbert to take her back.

"I'm sorry, but you know I can't," Ferbert would explain. This apology was always followed by, "When the time is right, you will see it again."

Eventually, Sophia stopped asking about the zoo. When she stopped asking about it, she stopped thinking about it. When she stopped thinking about it too, her mind focused on new things.

Ferbert taught her to read and write and about math, science, and geography. She filled her mind with the wonders and knowledge found between the covers of books, and as she filled her mind with new knowledge, her old memories, including those of the zoo, faded away.

In three years' time, she forgot everything about the zoo, the angry people, and the other children. She even forgot about Mayor Monev.

By the time she was seven years old, only three things occupied her mind: the two things she loved and one thing she wanted.

The first thing she loved was spending time with

her dad. She spent all day, every day, with Ferbert, and when they weren't reading in the high branches of the maple tree, they played games, ran outside, did cartwheels, played with dolls, and held tea parties. Sophia loved Ferbert as much as any daughter could love her father.

The second thing Sophia loved was learning and reading. She read about hundreds of different places, thousands of plants, and even more animals and insects. She read about great explorers and scientists and learned about faraway places and the great wonders of the world. There wasn't a subject Sophia didn't learn and didn't, in turn, love.

There was, however, the one thing she didn't have, and it was the one thing she wanted more than anything else: friends. Sophia wanted to play hide and seek, jump rope, and go on adventures with children her age; she wanted friends she could giggle with and tell secrets to. She knew that she would be the happiest girl in all the world if she made just one friend.

There was one problem, though: Sophia never went anywhere with other children. She'd read story after story about a place children gathered every day to learn and play and make friends: *school*. When she was five years old, she'd waited for Ferbert to send her to school, but he never did. The next year, when she was six years old, she'd waited again, but Ferbert never even mentioned school to Sophia. At seven years old, she didn't want to wait any longer and finally built up the courage to ask.

That fateful day was a month after Ferbert had given Sophia the yellow tulip, told her how he'd been to the Jumondo Forest, and realized that she had forgotten everything. They were sitting in the maple tree, reading. The summer was almost over, which meant the new school year would start soon.

"Dad, I have a question," Sophia announced.

"Oh yeah? What's that?" Ferbert looked up from his book.

"I was wondering if, maybe, I could… if you think it's a good idea that… I think I'm ready for… You know I'm old enough… I think it will be good for me if… I mean, I'm hoping—" As many words as Sophia knew, she couldn't find the right ones.

"Sophia," Ferbert interrupted, "if you want to ask something, just say it. If it's something good, how could I possibly say no?"

She sucked in a huge breath of air, held it for a few seconds, and then let her request burst out, "I want to go to school—a real school, with other kids!" Ferbert's eyebrows dropped, and he looked down at the book in his lap. Sophia's eyes stayed locked on his pained expression, which she had never seen before. "Dad, I'm sorry—forget it. I don't know what I was thinking. I don't need to go to school; I can learn everything I need from these books. It was a silly thing to ask."

Ferbert shook his head, "No, you're right. School will be good for you." He forced a smile and said,

"You can go."

Sophia smiled and tried to say thank you, but nothing came out.

FIRST DAY

"Today is going to be the best day of my life," Sophia announced on the first day of school, "but I'm a little nervous."

She and Ferbert sat at the breakfast table in the kitchen with Sophia shoveling spoonful after spoonful of cereal into her mouth and Ferbert reading the paper while eating toast.

"What could a girl as amazing as you be nervous about?" Ferbert's stomach twisted in knots as he thought about the past that Sophia had forgotten.

"I've never played with other kids. What if they

don't like me?"

Ferbert stopped eating and looked at his daughter with a loving smile. "Sophia, those other kids would be fools not to like you. Just remember that, sometimes, people don't see amazing things right away and often need a little time." He looked at his watch. "Oh, speaking of time, we need to get you out the door!"

She shoved the last two scoops of cereal into her mouth and slurped down the milk before jumping up from the table, grabbing her backpack, and running for the front door. She was halfway through the door when she froze.

"I forgot something," she announced as she turned around and ran toward Ferbert. Sophia jumped into his arms and hugged him, and he pulled her in tightly and returned the hug.

"Thank you so much, Dad," she gushed.

"You'd best get going if you're going to get to school on time." Ferbert loosened his hug. "No matter how things go today, remember that I love you."

"How could I ever forget?" Sophia turned and ran out the door.

She sprinted the whole way to school and arrived ten minutes before class was to begin. Kids ran around the field and played on the playground. At the far end of the field, a girl who looked to be Sophia's age tried to climb a tree without much success. Sophia ran to the young girl.

"Do you need some help?" she asked. "I'm really good at climbing trees."

The girl was smaller than Sophia, and her short, strawberry blonde hair extended just below her jaw with a slight curl at the ends. She turned around with tears rushing from her eyes, over her freckled cheeks, and to the edges of her quivering lips.

"One of the big kids threw my backpack in the tree," she whimpered, "but I can't climb trees."

"I'll help." Sophia didn't wait and started

climbing, swinging and jumping from branch to branch until she reached a baby blue backpack tangled in the branches. She carefully freed it of the tree's grasp and threw it over her shoulder, climbed down as easily as she climbed up, and handed the backpack to the young girl.

"That was amazing!" the girl screamed with delight.

"Nothing to it," Sophia smiled.

"I'm Bailey Cottonwood. What's your name?"

"I'm Sophia Fl—" A loud, ringing bell interrupted her.

"That means class is about to start," Bailey said. "Let's hurry so we can sit together." She grabbed Sophia by the hand and the two ran to their classroom. Bailey moved through the halls as if she had lived in the school her whole life and Sophia struggled to keep up. When they entered the room, Bailey looked around until she found two empty desks next to one another. "Hah, right up front. It'll be perfect!" Bailey exclaimed.

As they took their seats, Sophia felt as though she was going to burst with joy. Class hadn't even started and she already had a friend. She had not expected it to be so easy.

When everyone was seated, a woman wearing a plain dress with her hair pulled back in a bun walked to the front of the classroom. She planted her feet in front of Sophia and cleared her throat.

"I'm Mrs. Blantly, and I'll be your teacher this year," she announced. "Each day, I will call role. When I call your name, please say *here* and raise your hand." Mrs. Blantly put on her reading glasses, looked at her clipboard, and started calling out names in alphabetical order.

"Theodore Abbott?"

"Here," a dark-haired boy with thick glasses called.

"Gretchen Braunstein?"

"Here."

"Bailey Cottonwood?"

"Here."

Sophia sat up in her chair as the teacher neared her part of the alphabet.

"Garrett Dalton."

"Here."

"Samantha Farber?"

"Here."

Sophia listened intently for her name with her hand at the ready to announce her presence.

"Tommy Gladhill?"

Sophia's name wasn't called when it should have been. She continued listening carefully as other students' names were called.

When the teacher was finished, she looked up from her clipboard and asked, "Is there anyone whose name I didn't call?" Sophia raised her hand, and Mrs. Blantly smiled. "What's your name?"

Sitting up tall and proud she announced, "Sophia."

The woman took a quick glance at her clipboard and then looked back at the girl. "There is no Sophia on my list. What is your last name?"

Sophia sat up even taller and confidently announced, "Flembuzzle."

The room went perfectly still and silent; even Mrs. Blantly froze and her face went pale. She looked confused, frightened, and angry all at the same time, and Sophia looked around the room to discover everyone glaring at her with the same expression as the teacher.

Sophia slumped down in her chair. "Mrs. Blantly," she asked. "Did I do something wrong? What's the matter?"

The woman, however, didn't move or respond. Sophia turned toward her new friend, hoping to get some kind of answer, but Bailey was already collecting her school supplies and moving to a different seat. Sophia reached out and touched her arm.

"Don't touch me!" Bailey barked as she pulled away.

"But I thought we were friends?" Sophia pleaded.

The smaller girl stopped in her tracks, turned around, and glared at Sophia. "I will never be friends with a Flembuzzle. No one will ever be friends with you."

Tears pooled in Sophia's eyes and then rolled down her cheeks. She looked back to Mrs. Blantly. What was happening? Why had Bailey changed so quickly and why was Mrs. Blantly so upset?

Mrs. Blantly took a deep breath and commanded, "Sophia, go to the principal's office."

"What did I do?" Sophia quivered.

"Just go!"

PRINCIPAL'S OFFICE

Sophia sat on one side of the principal's enormous desk, and the principal, a frail looking man, with thick-framed glasses that appeared to be sturdier than him, sat on the other. She thought he had a pleasant face.

After studying her tear-stained cheeks and sniffling nose for a moment, he handed Sophia a tissue and introduced himself, "I'm Principal Winklestein. What's your name?"

"Sophia," she said, careful not to give her last name this time.

"Okay, Sophia," Principal Winklestein spoke with a nasally voice, "I know the first day of school can be rough. Why don't you just tell me what you did, and we'll get to work making you a better student and keeping you out of any more trouble."

"Trouble?" she asked. "I don't understand—I didn't do anything wrong."

"Young lady, teachers don't send students to see me unless they have done something wrong," the principal explained. "Now, tell me what you did and we can make things right."

"I promise, I didn't do anything wrong!" Sophia snapped. "Mrs. Blantly asked me my last name and I told her. I did exactly what she asked."

Principal Winklestein realized then that he didn't know her last name. "Okay. Let's start there. What is your last name?" Sophia pinched her lips shut at the question. "Sophia, I need you to tell me what you said to Mrs. Blantly," Principal Winklestein insisted. "What's your last name?"

She dropped her head and gazed at the floor. "Flembuzzle," Sophia muttered.

The mood in the room instantly changed, just as it had in the classroom. Sophia didn't look up, but she could feel the principal giving her the same look Mrs. Blantly had. After a long moment, Principal Winklestein stood and marched out of the office to the front desk, where his secretary sat.

Sophia turned around and peeked over the back of her chair. The door was cracked open just enough for Sophia to make out pieces of the conversation.

"I'm sure he'll want to know about this," he said.

"Do you think he'll be upset?" she asked.

"I suspect so." The secretary handed the phone to Principal Winklestein, who spoke for only a few minutes before handing it back. "He's on his way."

Sophia watched as the principal bit his fingernails and paced back and forth. Ten minutes later, two men approached the front desk. One of them was tall with broad shoulders and thin, long legs. The other was a short man with no distinct characteristics—the kind of man who blended into the crowd.

Sophia didn't recognize either man, but something about them seemed familiar. The principal approached the taller of the two and began speaking and pointing into his office. The taller man peered through the crack in the open door and made eye contact with Sophia, smiling and giving her a small wave with long, crooked, ugly fingers.

When the men headed toward the principal's office, Sophia ducked down in her seat. She didn't know why, but she suddenly felt scared and wanted to run or scream. The door squeaked open and she heard the thump of each footstep as it echoed through the room. She pinched her eyes shut as the thumping steps moved around the chair and stopped just in front of her. The only sound Sophia heard now was her own breathing.

The silence was broken by a gentle voice. "Sophia

68

Flembuzzle? It's okay to open your eyes—you're not in trouble."

Although there was something about this man Sophia did not like, she liked the way he talked to her: kind and soft. She opened her eyes and inched her head upward. The taller of the men was crouched in front of her chair, at her eye level.

"There's those beautiful eyes." He put a hand on Sophia's shoulder. "Let me introduce myself and my friend. I'm Mayor Max Monev and this is my assistant, Derek Dunger. You and I met a few years ago. Do you remember?"

She tried hard to remember but couldn't. She shook her head, and Mayor Monev smiled a sly, clever smile at Dunger.

"Sophia, Principal Winklestein told me what happened today. I bet you have a lot of questions."

She did have a lot of questions, but she remained silent. She gave the mayor a wide-eyed look and a slight nod to indicate she was listening but still deciding whether to trust him.

"Has anyone told you why people are acting so funny?"

Sophia shook her head. *Funny* is not the word she would've used.

The mayor tilted his head toward the principal. "Winklestein, I'm disappointed in you for leaving this poor girl in the dark. She deserves answers."

"I'm sorry, Mayor. I can explain it all now, if you'd like," the principal replied.

"No, I don't think that will be necessary. I have a better idea." The mayor stood. "It's easier to show than it is to tell, anyway. I say we take a little field trip."

"Of course," the principal gulped. "I can have someone bring one of the buses around."

"Certainly not! This girl deserves much better than an old, clunky bus for a field trip as important as this. I'll have Dunger bring the limousine around."

Sophia had never ridden in a limousine before. In fact, she had never even seen an actual limousine. She had only read about them and seen pictures. It was the kind of car a princess rode in.

Mayor Monev led her to the limousine, where Mr. Dunger opened the door.

"After you," he motioned and Sophia climbed in.

Before the mayor followed, he whispered to Dunger in a voice Sophia couldn't hear, "Are you sure this whole nice guy act is the way to go with this girl? She is a Flembuzzle, after all."

"Trust me, sir," Dunger responded without expression. "It'll work."

"It'd better work, or you'll be looking for a new job."

LIMOUSINE RIDE

Sophia stood in the limousine, half dazed, turning in circles with eyes as wide as silver dollars. The interior of the limousine was tall enough to stand up and long enough to do somersaults in—as big as Sophia's bedroom, but much fancier. She was still spinning in circles when Mayor Money sat by the door.

"If you take a seat, I'll show you the best part of the limo." He pointed to the seat by the opposite door. "Do you like soda-pop?"

"You have soda-pop?" Sophia asked as her tiny

body sank into the soft, leather seat.

"Darling, I don't just have soda-pop; I have a whole soda-pop machine!" the mayor opened a console between their seats.

Inside were glass cups, ice, and a short hose with a funny-looking nozzle on the end. He filled a cup with ice and filled it with soda-pop by pressing a button on the back of the nozzle. He dropped a straw into the fizzing drink and then handed it to Sophia.

"Thank you." She sipped from the glass as the limousine began to move. "I've never seen anything this fancy before."

"Well, I take good care of this town, so they take care of me." Mayor Monev closed the console. "The people here are hard-working and trusting. In fact, they will trust just about anyone—sometimes even those they shouldn't." As if he were reading her thoughts, he then said, "You probably don't believe me, because no one has treated you very well today.

Am I right?"

She nodded and took another sip of her soda-pop.

"Well, you have to understand something. The worst thing someone can do to good, trusting people is to betray that trust—to take advantage of their kindness. When someone betrays trust, it's hard for the victim to trust the next person who comes along. That doesn't make the victim bad; it's just human nature. The person who betrays trust, on the other hand—that's a different story." Mayor Monev stared out the window as he spoke, "Everyone at that school is a good person, but they are also victims. They don't trust you because of a man who betrayed them all three years ago."

Sophia remained suspicious of the mayor. In her mind, there was zero reason for anyone to treat her so poorly. "I don't understand why they would be mean to me if it was someone else that hurt them," she said.

Mayor Monev rolled down her window and motioned for her to look outside. She saw empty houses, empty restaurants, empty schools, empty hotels, and empty businesses. Most of the windows and doors were boarded up, and tall weeds covered the yards and grew through every crack in the sidewalks, driveways, and parking lots. Spider webs and dust covered the entrances, and the only sign of life were the rats scurrying into the shadows as the limousine passed.

"Why are they empty?" Sophia asked. "Why are you showing this to me?"

"Excellent questions. It is because of that man I mentioned. When he moved to Vedner he told us he was building the most exotic zoo in the world. He told me and everyone here that people would come from all around the world to see his zoo, and he demanded we quadruple the size of our town."

A feeling in Sophia's gut told her something was not right about the mayor's story, but she was anxious to hear the rest and ignored that feeling.

"I thought it was a bad idea," he continued, "but the people of Vedner trusted that man and spent almost all of their money building what you see. They even threw a big party in the man's honor, but he refused to come! On the day he opened his zoo, he made us give him the last of our money before we learned it was all a lie."

"That's terrible," Sophia responded.

The limousine zigged and zagged up a windy road before coming to a stop, and Mayor Monev motioned for her to look out the window again. They were parked in front of a towering gate—the same gate that Sophia could see from the maple tree. She had no memory of being up close like this before; it was a spectacular sight.

"Do you recognize this gate?" the mayor asked.

"Yes, sir. I can see it from the maple tree my dad and I climb," Sophia said.

"Of course you can—it can be seen from every

part of Vedner. Do you remember the day you went through the gate?"

"My dad told me I went inside once, but I don't remember."

"Sophia, the day you went inside was the day I met you," Mayor Monev explained. "Are you sure you don't remember that? Your father didn't tell you what happened that day?"

"Honest, sir, I don't remember anything," she answered. "I asked my dad about it this summer, but he didn't want to talk about it."

"Can't say I'm surprised." Dunger and the mayor exchanged sly looks that tried to hide their excitement at Sophia's answer. "If I were him, I wouldn't want my daughter to know, either." She gave the mayor a curious glare as he continued, "It was an awful day when we learned the truth about the man and the zoo. You see, when we went through this gate, we discovered there were no animals inside. A zoo without a single animal—can you imagine? Well, I kindly asked the man for an explanation, and he told us we were blind fools and then cast some kind of spell on the children to make them think they were seeing animals that weren't there, turning the children against their parents and trying to split families apart."

Mayor Monev put his hands on his chest in a big show. "It broke my heart, but I had to protect our families. I had no choice but to lock the gate and forbid anyone from going into that place ever again. You were one of the children there that day—you were one of the children I had to protect." He paused for a moment. "Of course, the people here never forgot the awful things that man did. But I can't blame them, especially after how long they had to wait for the man's spells to wear off. It was only recently that your classmates were able to see the truth. That man," Mayor Monev said with a dramatic sigh, "is the reason everyone treats you so terribly."

"Mr. Mayor, I don't understand," Sophia said. "What does this awful man have to do with me?"

"It pains me to tell you this, but that… what did you call him? An *awful man*? Well, that awful man is your father, Mr. Ferbert Flembuzzle."

Sophia threw her hands over her mouth. She couldn't believe that her father would do such a thing, and she couldn't believe she had called her father an awful man! "You're lying!" she screamed. "My dad would never trick anyone or do any of those things! My dad is the best man in the whole world!"

Mayor Monev faked a sympathetic smile. "Sophia, I understand why you don't want to believe me. No one wants to believe their father can do bad things, but you said it yourself; you don't remember. Surely, you are not suggesting that you know more than the hundreds of people that do remember. I'm sorry you had to learn the truth this way. I'm sorry that your father kept this hidden from you."

Sophia didn't know what to say. She wanted to tell the mayor he and everyone else was wrong, but the words wouldn't come. She had no way to prove it; all she knew was that she didn't want to hear any more.

She scrunched her eyes together, tightened her lips, and sat in silence until they returned to school. As they drove, a horrible thought that made her stomach turn entered Sophia's mind. She winced and tried to push it out of her head, but the thought remained. *What if Mayor Monev was telling the truth? What if that was the reason Ferbert didn't tell her about the zoo?*

When the limousine pulled up to the school, she threw open the door and jumped out before the vehicle came to a stop.

"I don't think she believed me," Mayor Monev told Dunger when she was gone.

"I didn't expect her to," he responded. "At least, not today."

"Really? Then remind me why you think it's such a great idea to be kind to that rotten, little twerp."

"It's easy to distrust someone unkind but quite difficult to remain suspicious of those who are nice. Now, every time someone is cruel to her, she will think about how kind you were to tell her the things her own father wouldn't. With pesky thoughts like that rolling around a lonely girl's head for long enough and even she won't trust her father."

SOPHIA'S ARMOR

When Sophia returned to the classroom, Mrs. Blantly was writing math problems on the board. Sophia shuffled toward the front of the classroom to where she'd sat that morning, but her desk was gone. She looked for another place to sit, but all the seats were taken.

Sophia turned toward Mrs. Blantly, desperate to understand, but the woman only gave her a crusty glare and pointed to the back of the classroom. Tucked away, in the darkest corner, facing the back wall, was a solitary desk—Sophia's desk. Her shoulders dropped and she lowered her head as she lurched across the room, the other children sneering at her as she took her seat.

During the math lesson, Sophia turned around to see what was on the board until Mrs. Blantly yelled at her. "Stop climbing on the desk like it's a jungle gym!" So, the girl turned back around and sat in silence until the bell rang, indicating the end of the school day.

Her walk home was long and slow, but her mind was restless. "Tomorrow will be different. Tomorrow, I will make friends," she told herself. "The mayor is wrong about my dad."

Saying it out loud helped, but the thought in the back of Sophia's mind remained. *What if the mayor is telling the truth?*

Those pesky thoughts stirred in her brain until she reached the front porch of her small home. She walked through the door with her head down, staring at her feet.

"How was my girl's first day?" Ferbert asked from where he sat at the table. He raised his arm, which held the canvas satchel. "What do you say we head out to the maple and do a little reading, and you can tell me all about the things you learned and the friends you made?"

When Sophia lifted her head, her tear-stained cheeks and puffy, red eyes told him everything. He dropped the satchel, jumped to his feet, and wrapped his arms around his daughter.

"Dad, I didn't make any friends." Her breath was short and jumpy as she sobbed. "I don't know why I thought anyone was going to like me."

"Don't worry; you'll make friends. In time, you will." Ferbert pulled away just enough to see her face. "The roughest roads often lead to the most spectacular destinations."

One side of Sophia's mouth lifted with a slight hint of a smile. "You're probably right."

"Now, are you ready for a foot race to the

maple?"

Sophia shrugged. "I think I'm just gonna go read in my room, if that's okay."

Ferbert's brows dropped and his eyes turned soft. His daughter had never said no to reading in the maple tree. "Of course that's okay."

Sophia went to her room, shut the door, and stayed there until the next morning.

At breakfast, she poked at her scrambled eggs with her fork. She didn't cut them, stir them, scoop, or eat them—just poked.

"It's not alive; no need to stab it to death," her dad said with a playful grin.

Ferbert had been sitting at the table all morning, but Sophia looked up with a frozen, wide-eyed expression of someone who was surprised to learn she wasn't alone.

She forced a smile and put down her fork. "I guess… I'm just not that hungry."

Sophia waited nervously for him to ask why, but he didn't. There was no need—he knew. Instead, he gave a gentle smile and looked at his watch.

"Jumpin' jellyfish!" Ferbert exclaimed. "We need to get you out the door or you'll be late."

Sophia rose like a zombie and Ferbert walked beside her as she staggered toward the door. She lifted her backpack from its hook and pulled it onto her back, and just before stepping out the door, Ferbert pulled her in for a hug.

Sophia didn't want him to let go because the end of the hug meant the beginning of her journey to the place where everyone seemed to hate her. Ferbert didn't want to let go either. His heart ached at the thought of letting his daughter go somewhere that caused so much pain, but he knew it was necessary and eventually released her from his loving embrace.

When she arrived at school, Sophia found children playing tag in the field and zipping across the playground, but it wasn't long before she felt them staring at her. She spotted Bailey playing with a group of girls near the monkey bars. They kept glancing in Sophia's direction, until she made eye contact with the strawberry blonde girl. Sophia was shocked when Bailey waved for her to come over.

Maybe she wants to say sorry, she wondered. *Maybe she still wants to be friends.*

Sophia hesitated for only a moment before walking to the group.

"Hi, Bailey. I just wanted to say—" She stopped when they started whispering, giggling, and snickering with one another and an awful feeling came over Sophia. The girls shushed each other and then, in unison, they burst into a loud chant.

There once was a man who lied, lied, lied.
He had a silly daughter who cried, cried, cried.
If you get the chance, and I hope you do,
push her in the mud or she'll lie to you, too.

At once, the girls lunged forward and shoved Sophia, who stumbled and fell backward into a deep puddle of mud. Thick, dirty filth splashed in all directions and globs of mud crashed down on Sophia's head and face. The scene around her erupted into chaos.

A giant crowd of children gathered around her. Some of them pointed and laughed so hard that their heads tipped backward, their mouths agape. Others laughed so hard that they collapsed to the ground. It seemed as though the world started to spin around the mud-covered girl as shrieking laughter exploded from every mouth. Sophia closed her eyes and threw her hands over her ears. The laughter continued until the bell rang. The laughter faded, and soon she sat in complete silence. Hesitantly, she opened her eyes and rose to her feet. She was alone.

Any other time in Sophia's life, she would have run home and told her dad what happened, knowing he would wrap his arms around her and tell her everything was going to be okay. Today was different, though. For the first time, Sophia felt both alone and afraid. She thought about what the mayor said and worried that not even her dad would understand.

She stood in the mud puddle with her head down, looking at her legs and arms. She watched as the warm sun dried the mud and transformed it into a hard crust over her skin, reminding her of the armor-like shell of the Brazilian three-banded armadillo.

Sophia took a breath, wiped the tears from her face, and clenched her jaw. "That's it. I will be like the armadillo to protect myself," she said to herself. "I just need to make myself tough." As she said it, she felt a dark, cold, invisible armor mold and wrap around her heart. When it was done she didn't feel sadness anymore.

Sophia went to her classroom, confident that no cruel words or nasty acts were going to penetrate her heart anymore, and took her seat facing the back corner.

At lunch, she had nowhere to sit. As she passed by each table, the children sneered, "No Flembuzzles allowed here." The only place Sophia was permitted to sit was on the floor next to the trash cans. No one bothered her until the end of lunch, when the other children went to throw away their leftovers. "Oops," they blurted sarcastically as they dumped food on her head and laughed.

Elmer, the janitor, watched and then grumbled to Sophia, "I ain't cleaning that mess up—you were the last one to touch it."

Instead of jumping rope, swinging on the monkey bars, or playing kickball at recess, Sophia hid in the high branches of the tree she'd climbed to retrieve Bailey's backpack.

When teams were being picked during gym class, Sophia was not the last kid picked. Rather, she wasn't picked at all. The teacher and all the students acted as though she were invisible and started the game without her.

When she asked which team she was on, the gym teacher scowled at her with his sharp eyes and huffed, "I'll have none of your backtalk. You take that untamed mouth of yours straight to principal's office." He shook his head and continued, "If I were Principal Winklestein, I'd kick you out of this school."

Sophia went without a word.

"The only reason I'm not kicking you out of school," Principal Winklestein started, "is because Mayor Monev forbade me from doing so. I don't want a Flembuzzle in my office, so go back to class."

Back in class, Sophia completed her classwork perfectly, but Mrs. Blantly plastered her assignments with giant frowny faces and Zs.

"What does a Z mean?" Sophia asked.

"It means your work was the worst I've seen," Mrs. Blantly responded. "It was so bad that I had to skip F and go straight to the end of the alphabet. Now, go to the principal for back-talking me."

Sophia spent nearly all day being sent back and forth between class and the principal's office, and when school got out, she walked home with her face to the ground the whole way.

Ferbert sat at the table when she walked through the door. He smiled but didn't ask how her day was, as he could already tell by Sophia's slumped shoulders and drooping head.

"Can I interest you in an afternoon in the maple tree?" he asked with a gentle smile. "An afternoon in the maple always makes you feel better."

She wanted to pour out her heart and tell him everything, but she couldn't. Her heart ached as she realized that the invisible armor she had put on not only blocked cruelty, but it also blocked love and kindness. She no longer felt sad or happy. No, it was something much worse: she felt nothing.

"No thanks," was all Sophia could muster before shuffling off to her room.

THE BOOK

The next day at school, Sophia made some minor adjustments but maintained her invisible armor. She never turned around in her seat to see the board, and when she sat by the trashcans at lunch, she ate so fast that she barely chewed, ensuring she was done before the other kids could dump food on her. At recess, she went straight to the tree and hid in the high branches, and in PE, she sat under the bleachers when teams were picked and never asked which one she was on. She continued doing all her classwork but stopped asking about her Zs. Soon, her teachers and classmates barely paid Sophia any attention. She became nearly as invisible as her armor.

Every day, when Sophia returned home from school, Ferbert sat at that table and invited her to read in the maple tree. Every day, however, Sophia declined his offer before retiring to her room.

Days, weeks, and months passed until the night Sophia discovered the book that changed everything.

She was sitting in her bed, looking at a calendar and counting the days since Mayor Monev had given her a ride in his limousine. She had almost made it through the entire school year and was now only a month away from her eighth birthday.

She looked at her clock: it was late and she should have been asleep already, but she suddenly felt thirsty. She put down the calendar and went to the kitchen to get a drink, and as she passed the hall, she saw a light on in Ferbert's office. Curious, she tip-toed down the hallway and peered through the open door. Ferbert sat at his desk hunched over a book with his back to her.

It was a book she had never seen before. It was hand written and had a leather cover with tattered, worn corners. The pages were thick and crimped from water damage. It was old and beat up, but something about it seemed precious and valuable.

As she watched Ferbert read, she thought about all the afternoons she'd spent in her room instead of reading in the maple tree with him. She wished there was a way to get those afternoons back; she didn't want to miss any more.

I should talk to him, Sophia thought. *I should tell him about everything at school and how I want to go back to the way things were.*

As she debated what to say and how to say it, Ferbert removed his reading glasses and sat up in his chair. Sophia watched in silence as he picked up the book, placed it in the bottom drawer of his desk, and locked the drawer with a key. He placed the key underneath the lamp on his desk, stood, and started turning to leave. Fearing she had seen something she was not meant to see, Sophia slid behind the door and waited there until her dad walked out of the room and turned off the light.

When Sophia was certain he had gone to bed, she tip-toed through the dark office, lifted the lamp, and picked up the key. She unlocked the bottom drawer with a soft click. The drawer made a faint rubbing noise as she pulled it open. Goosebumps raced up her arm as her fingertips touched the leather cover and pulled the book into the crook of her arm.

She closed the drawer, hurried back to her room, and hid under her covers with a small reading light, where she examined the book. She thought about how her dad kept it locked up. Who was he hiding it from? Why was he hiding it at all? Sophia felt a tinge of panic when she considered the possibility that it might contain awful secrets—secrets that might confirm all those horrible things Mayor Monev had told her.

Hesitantly, she pulled open the front cover with her thumb and hesitation transformed into confusion as she began reading.

Step One: Find the right tree. Not all Jumondo trees will share their sap. (Note: Finding the right tree is a matter of luck.)

Step Two: Climb to the first branch. (Note: Only the best climbers should attempt this.)

Step Three: Place the pointed end of the sap-tap against the trunk directly above the first branch. (Note: This is the only part of the tree weak enough to get a wooden sap-tap through the thick bark.)

Step Four: Hammer the sap-tap into the trunk by striking it five times. (Note: The first four must be gentle and the fifth must be as hard as you can.)

It was clear these were instructions for getting sap

from Jumondo trees, but for what purpose? Sophia had read all about them but had never heard of anyone getting sap from the trees. She wondered if it meant anything at all as she continued to the next page, which began with a short message in different handwriting—Ferbert's handwriting.

This book contains the most spectacular events of my life. These events are unbelievable but all true. Don't read this unless you are capable of believing in the unbelievable.

Sophia paused before continuing to the next page. She had no idea if she was capable of believing the unbelievable. For a moment, she thought about closing the book and putting it back, but a small part of her seemed to be saying, "Keep reading."

Taking a deep breath, she turned the page.

THE JUMONDO FOREST

The day I graduated from high school, I went to the bank. Every penny I had ever earned was deposited there, and that day, I took it all out and closed my account. I packed up everything I needed for a trip around the world, kissed my mother, hugged my father, and left the only home I had ever known.

From the day I was born until that day, the very normal town of Medockery had been my home. I had been waiting my whole life for the day I could leave—I just didn't belong.

When most people say they don't belong somewhere, it's usually because they have a case of the toos. That is, they think too highly or too little of themselves. Those who think too highly of themselves leave their homes because they think they are too big, too smart, too important, too talented—they hope to find other people who match their size, intelligence, importance, and talents and assume these new people will be more deserving of their company.

On the other side are the people who think too little of themselves. These people spend their lives feeling too small, too dumb, or too unimportant and run away in hopes of finding a place with smaller people who don't know as much and are less important than the people in their home town. That way, they will finally feel bigger, smarter, and more important.

I did not have a case of the toos. I never felt too big or too small; I had a case of the just rights. My whole life, I always felt I was just the right size, had just the right intelligence, and was just the right importance.

All of this made for a very comfortable but boring life. There was no reason to leave, but I felt something calling to me. I didn't know what it was, but I knew I was meant to leave my comfortable life and discover spectacular things. So,

I left. I didn't know what I was searching for, but I searched everywhere.

I traveled thousands of miles by plane, boat, car, horseback, helicopter, raft, hang glider, camelback, and foot. I traveled east and west, north and south, up and down, over and under, in and out, around and between. I faced rainstorms, snow storms, hail storms, thunderstorms, ice storms, sand storms, and dust storms. I endured earthquakes, tornados, hurricanes, and typhoons. I traveled to places few dared to go.

I waded through the crocodile and snake-infested Verplickitty Swamp. I huffed my way across the Drobwobble Desert. I stood at the edge of the Rumgumhum Canyon. I trekked the Blorterblum Wilderness and scaled the highest parts of the Swidwiggy Falls. I searched the Wungleswarp Jungle, the Tuffscrumble Tundra, the Zaflupert Plains, the Pogsfurful Tropics, the Hamthudry Islands, the Capperskoppy Caverns, the Fremwemmy Wetlands, the Nocarogubby Mountains, and many more places. I saw impressive scenes, beautiful birds, ferocious mammals, peculiar insects, and calming landscapes, but I didn't find what I was meant to discover. I continued until I arrived at the Jumondo Forest, and it was there that I had my first true, yet unbelievable, discovery.

The forest was covered with Jumondo trees—trees so big they take a full day to climb and a full minute to run all the way around. The thick bark appears soft to the eye, but feels as hard as steel, and twists up the length of the trunk as if it had been placed there by a tornado. At the top, massive branches jut out in all directions covered by bold, green leaves as wide as a man's arm is long. The trees are amazing, but not unbelievable.

I considered exploring the forest, but I was hungry and tired, so I sat down, opened my travel bag, and started digging for food. All I had left was a single slice of bread, so I leaned against the tree and nibbled the bread, trying to make it last. As I ate, my fatigue took over and, before I knew it, I had fallen asleep.

I was woken by a sound from a nearby Jumondo tree of a

man climbing down and grumbling to himself. The man wore pants covered in patches (though, truthfully, they were more patch than pants), held up by an old, frayed rope. His hair was dirty and long, and his beard was tangled and covered with old bits of food and twigs. Over his shoulder, the man carried a satchel of some sort with a bucket hanging from it. I watched in curiosity as the man reached the forest floor, and when he saw me, he walked right up and stood in front of me. He seemed to study me for several minutes before speaking.

"367 months since I got it right," the man ranted. "Over 30 years of searching and nothing. I quit. I quit. I quit."

He then threw the satchel and bucket on the ground at my feet.

"I'm sorry, sir. I don't underst—"

"It's yours. It's all yours, but I warn you: it's a curse." The man didn't wait for a reply and cackled as he ran off. Like a ghost, he disappeared into the forest.

I opened the satchel and found a homemade hammer—a rock lashed between two sticks. I also found two ropes, a knife, a leather-bound book, a small bottle labeled Jumondo

Syrup, *and a hollow stick with one end carved into a sharp point and the other curving downward, giving it the appearance of a wooden faucet.*

As I examined the strange device, I noticed something peculiar. Carved into the side were the letters F.F.—my initials. At first, I was amused by the coincidence, but then I got a strange feeling it was not a coincidence. This device was meant for me—it had always been meant for me.

My stomach gurgled and wobbled, demanding food. Without a second thought, I opened the bottle labeled Jumondo Syrup, *only to be disappointed. Except for a single drop, it was empty. After examining the meager contents, I lifted the bottle to my lips, closed my eyes, and tipped it. When the single drop then slid off the edge of the bottle and landed on my tongue, my taste buds went crazy.*

"Wow," I called out. "That's delicious!"

Was this what that man had spent 30 years searching for? I moved on to the next item, the leather-bound book. I thumbed through the pages and discovered there was only writing on the first page: instructions for how to get Jumondo *sap from a Jumondo tree.*

Sophia paused and flipped back to the first page, where she reread the steps, before continuing.

It seemed I had everything I needed to collect Jumondo sap, so I determined I would give it a go.

I looked around, considering which tree was the right tree, but then I realized that, if it was a matter of luck, there didn't seem to be any sense in searching too hard. I turned around and stared straight up the trunk of the tree I had been resting against. By falling asleep against this tree, I had been lucky enough to encounter the strange man and end up with a sap-tap, and while the tree didn't seem any more special than any other tree, it had been lucky so far.

I stuffed everything back into the satchel, threw it over my shoulder, and climbed for hours and hours before I reached the first branch. When I did, I straddled the branch like a man riding a horse, pulled out the sap-tap and hammer, and proceeded to give the sap-tap four gentle hits. I then raised the hammer and brought it down as hard as I could. There was a loud thud, but that was not the only noise. The thud was followed by a loud, bird like shriek that rang through the air and rattled my ear drums.

I dropped the hammer and threw my hands over my ears. Without warning, the tree started shaking. The branches bounced up and down and bent back and forth. I let go of my ears and grabbed hold of the sap-tap, which was still stuck in the bark and held on with all my might as the shaking grew more and more violent. A splintering noise erupted from the base of the tree. Looking down, I saw the trunk of the tree splitting in half, right up the middle, and spread upward, stopping only a few feet below the branch I sat on. Half of the trunk pulled out of the ground like a leg stuck in mud. Dirt-covered roots dangled above the surface for only a moment before crashing back down, and then the other half of the trunk did the same.

The tree began twisting back and forth with such force that my feet flew outward. I grasped the sap-tap and squeezed until my knuckles turned white, but the twisting intensified and my grip failed me. My body was thrown through the air and smashed into a neighboring Jumondo tree, where I landed on one of its branches.

After recovering from my crash, I watched the rest of the scene unfold from my new location. One branch on each side of the twisting tree stretched outward like massive, leaf-covered wings and flapped. Another branch shot upward, like the neck of a giraffe, and I realized it was where the horrible shriek was coming from. This branch was shaped like the head of an ostrich with a tuft of leaves sprouting from the top like an umbrella.

The tree pivoted its body and its head swung toward me until its beak pressed against the tip of my nose and split open, revealing its enormous, hollow mouth. I threw my arms over my head in a useless effort to protect myself, as I waited to be swallowed whole, but I only felt warm air rush over my body as the creature let out another painful shriek.

When the shriek stopped, the creature closed its mouth and tucked its wings close to its body, and using its tree trunk legs, it ran deep into the Jumondo Forest. I watched in awe as the

giant Jumondo bird bobbed between the other trees as it ran
out of sight.

Sophia was still hiding under her covers and turning the page when she thought she heard something. She poked her head out from the covers to investigate and didn't hear any more noises but discovered her room was no longer dark. Morning sunlight shone through her bedroom window. Sophia looked at the clock: it was 6:59 A.M.

Ferbert's alarm clock went off every day at 7:00 A.M., and at 7:01 A.M., he always poked his head into Sophia's room to make sure she was awake.

Sophia leapt out of her bed and raced down the hall on the tips of her toes, sailed into Ferbert's study, and placed the book back in its proper drawer. Without making a sound, she locked the drawer and returned the key to its rightful place, raced back to her bed, flew under the covers, and pretended to be sleeping. Seconds later, Ferbert pressed the door open.

"Sophia, it's time to get up."

She stretched out her arms, pretending she was waking from a long sleep, but her heart pounded so hard that it felt as though it was going to leap out of her chest. "Okay, Dad. I'm getting up."

THE ZOO

Sophia ate her breakfast in silence, as she always did, but on this morning, she fought the urge to ask the hundreds of questions bouncing through her head. If she asked any questions about the Jumondo bird, it would surely reveal that she had taken and read Ferbert's book—an act she did not want her father to know about.

He had shared every book he owned with Sophia, but not this one. It was clear to Sophia that he didn't want anyone reading it, and she assumed that if he knew she had, he would surely hide it somewhere new. If Sophia was going to continue reading the book, it was crucial her dad didn't know.

Since asking Ferbert was not an option, she needed to get answers some other way.

Sophia finished her breakfast and stepped outside to begin her long walk. She looked in the direction of the school and then up the zig-zag road that led to the massive gate at the top of the hill. Just beyond the gate was the massive Jumondo tree.

After considering her options for only a moment, Sophia ran as fast as she could to the long, zig-zag road. At the top, she stood in the shadow of the towering gate. Over the years, thick vines had woven their way between the curved, elaborate metal bars to the point that the gate appeared to be more plant than metal. Hanging on the gate was a sign partially covered by the vines. She pushed them aside and read:

THIS IS NOT A ZOO.
NO ONE ALLOWED INSIDE.

Sophia shook her head and let the vines drop back in front of the lettering. She didn't care what the sign said—it was not going to stop her from getting answers.

She pulled on the gate with all her might, but it didn't move. Sophia then pushed with all her strength. Again, no movement. She shook the gate furiously, but it didn't budge. After pacing up and down the vine covered wooden fence on each side of the gate, she found a section with loose boards. She wedged a stick between the boards and popped one free from its bottom nail. The board now swung freely from side to side by its top nail. Sophia pushed it aside and wedged her way through the tight opening. Once inside, she sprinted toward the massive Jumondo tree in the center of the zoo.

The sign indicated it was the giant Jumondo bird exhibit, and from the waist high barrier, Sophia studied the trunk and branches of the massive tree.

She scanned every part of it, looking for some sign that it was alive—some sign that it might be the creature from Ferbert's book. She looked for a crack where the trunk might separate into two legs and watched the branches to see if there was any movement, but she couldn't see any evidence that this tree was a bird or any other kind of creature.

"I need to be closer," she mumbled as she climbed over the barrier and entered the exhibit.

At the base of the tree, she pressed her hand against the thick bark that twisted up the trunk and had the sudden urge to climb. Almost reflexively, she started her ascent up the tree until she reached the first branch, out of breath and exhausted.

Sophia could see all of Vedner from where she sat, including her school, where the kids were loading into buses and leaving. Had it really been that long? Had she been climbing for the entire school day? A fleeting sense of guilt and worry entered her mind. She had missed the entire day of school. What would her dad say? How much trouble would she be in? As quickly as the concern entered her mind, however, it exited. She was so ignored at school that it was doubtful anyone had even noticed her absence.

Sophia leaned back against the tree as she took in the view and felt something jab her in the back. She whipped around to see a stick protruding from the bark. It was hollow and shaped like a faucet.

"The sap-tap?" she remembered, smiling, as she examined it more closely. She found two letters carved into the side and traced them with her finger. "F.F.," she whispered to herself with growing excitement.

Although she didn't see the tree come to life and run around, something marvelous happened as Sophia traced her father's initials. It wasn't anything a person could see, but something in her heart that could only be felt. It was the feeling that her heart knew something that her brain didn't understand. In that moment, the invisible armor she had been wearing all year grew a little softer.

Sophia realized Ferbert would soon wonder where she was, so she raced down the tree, which was much easier and faster than going up, and sprinted home.

When she arrived, Ferbert was already setting the table for dinner. She realized she had no valid excuse for her late return, but to her surprise, her dad didn't even mention it.

"Hungry?" he asked with a gentle smile.

"Yes, I'm starving," Sophia replied, not realizing that, for the first time since being pushed in the mud, she actually smiled.

DROBWOBBLE DESERT

Sophia fought to keep her eyelids open during dinner as she mindlessly scooped food into her mouth. The only thing keeping her awake was the thought of getting her hands back on her dad's hidden book, but she also knew that she needed sleep. The problem was that the only time she could read it was when Ferbert was asleep, which was unfortunately the same time *she* was supposed to be asleep. As she mechanically chewed her food, she devised a step by step plan:

(1)   Go to bed right after dinner and sleep.

(2)   Set an alarm for midnight and sneak into Ferbert's study and retrieve the book.

(3)   Reset the alarm for 6:55 A.M. (five minutes before the time Ferbert woke each day) and start reading.

(4)   Return book to the locked drawer.

(5)   Go back to bed and pretend to be sleeping when Ferbert comes in at 7:01 A.M.

Sophia swallowed the last of her dinner and announced, "I'm pretty tired; I think I'm gonna go to bed."

"Well, you do look zapped," Ferbert said. "Are you feeling alright?"

"Oh… yeah, school is just… uh…" Sophia struggled to find the right words. "I'm feeling fine—just tired, that's all."

At midnight, Sophia was woken by the sound of

her alarm. Just as she'd planned, she retrieved Ferbert's book and hid under her sheets. She fanned through the pages until she found where she'd left off the night before.

After the giant Jumondo bird ran off into the distance, I didn't know what to do with myself. A tree that seemed no different than any other had turned out to be a spectacular creature, and I almost missed it. What if I had made the same mistake everywhere else? Were there other creatures as fantastic as the giant Jumondo bird? Had I just failed to open my eyes?

I decided to return to each nook and cranny of the world, but this time, I would open my eyes and see things for what they were. I gathered my belongings, including the satchel and its remaining contents, and restarted my journey. My first stop was back to the Drobwobble Desert.

To get there, I took a two-week boat trip across an ocean. At a small port town, I purchased a camel and searched for a guide to take me through the desert. This proved to be more difficult than my previous visit, as I was told this was the Season of the Angry Sands.

"You must wait three months until the Season of the Angry Sands is over. If you don't wait, the sand storms will kill you—they kill everyone in their path," each guide told me.

I couldn't wait three months, though. I had been called to the Drobwobble Desert and something told me that, if I waited as the guides suggested, it would be too late.

With no willing guide, I had no choice but to venture into the desert on my own. I loaded my camel with all my belongings, tied them down, and threw the satchel containing the book over my shoulder. The locals begged me not to go, but I explained that I had to.

Before leaving, the most frightened of the guides grabbed me by the arm and whispered in my ear, "Mr. Ferbert, all that awaits you is your own death." The man's warning was solemn. "During the Season of the Angry Sands, there is no way to predict when the deathly sand storms will attack. You may not see one for a month, or you may be consumed by one this very night. You will not know when the storm is coming until you see it." The man grabbed the top of my head and rotated it toward the desert, pointing to the horizon with his other hand. "The horizon will be peaceful and calm, and with a single blink of your eye, the terrible storm will appear. If you can see it, it's already too late—the storms are impossible to outrun and the desert provides no shelter strong enough. The storm will rip trees out of the sand, tear tents to pieces, and even turn stone buildings to rubble. If you see a storm, you are already dead."

I was sure those guides had good reason to be frightened, but they had not seen the magnificent, as I had. They had not stood face to face with the giant Jumondo bird, and I just knew that somewhere in the Drobwobble Desert was a creature just as fantastic.

Of course, I didn't know anything about the creature awaiting me. I didn't know what it looked like, where to find it, or if it was friendly or dangerous. I only knew that it, whatever it was, was out there, and all I could do was hope I found it before the sand storms found me.

I journeyed deep into the Drobwobble Desert and trekked over endless hills of sand. During the day, the heat from the sun burned down relentlessly, sucking the moisture right out of me. At night, the cold desert air robbed me of body heat. Still, each morning, I loaded my belongings and climbed on top of my camel. Every day, I traveled deeper and deeper into the desert, always keeping a keen eye on my surroundings.

After two weeks of searching, I saw nothing but miles and miles of sand in every direction. For three weeks, I saw no creatures—not even a single insect. Luckily, I also saw no storm on the horizon.

When I was hundreds of miles from civilization, I saw the first sign of life—a creature that changed everything. The sighting was at the end of a long day of travel, after the sun had set. Under the light of the moon and stars, I stopped and prepared for the night. I jumped off the camel and began untying my gear which was secured to the camel's back by the two ropes found in the satchel, but I soon discovered that the knot in the first rope required significant effort to loosen.

I grabbed it with both hands and pulled with all my arm

strength—nothing. Using the full weight of my body, I leaned back and pulled again—still nothing. I then leveraged my feet against the camel, who only looked at me with bored indifference as I pulled back a final time with all my might.

The knot finally broke free, and I flopped backward and somersaulted across the desert floor. Looking up and spitting sand from my mouth, I saw that my tent, food, and canteens dangled from the other rope still lashed around the camel. I stood and shook the sand off, and prepared to conquer the second rope when I saw movement under the sand, near the camel's back foot. I dropped to my hands and knees and watched with hopes that this was the beginning of something great, but the next minute a scorpion popped out of the sand—a normal-sized, mundane, boring scorpion. I told myself it was a mistake to get excited, but then it did something I was not ready for.

The scorpion zipped across the sand and, without warning, it thrust its stinger over its body and into the camel's foot. A painful scream exploded from the camel, and it burst into a sprint, my tent, food, and water still dangling from the other rope.

I leapt to my feet and, in a mad dash, raced after it, but it was no use—the camel was too fast. My mad dash slowed to a sprint, a run, a jog, a walk, and then a stand-still. I fell to my knees as I watched the camel disappear into the moonlit night with my tent, food, and water. With only the clothes on my back and the satchel, I collapsed into the sand and passed out from exhaustion.

I awoke to the sound of a faint buzz and a sting on the back of my neck. Instinctually, my hand zoomed upward and slapped the attacker, and I examined my hand to see the smashed remains of a mosquito smeared across my palm.

A mosquito in the middle of the dry desert? It seemed impossible—mosquitos need a water source to survive.

I sat upright in the sand to see a single set of tracks ahead of me: the camel's. Behind me, I saw two sets of tracks coming toward me: mine and the camel's. To my left, there was nothing but sand, but to my right, I saw a tiny, green dot in the distance. I scrambled to my feet and squinted. Was it an oasis or just a mirage? It was too far away for me to be sure.

If I followed the tracks, I might catch the camel and my gear, which could be the difference between life and death. If the dot was not an oasis, I would die chasing a mirage. I took a final look at the smashed mosquito on the palm of my hand and decided to head for the green speck.

Too tired to lift my feet, I dragged them through the sand. The green speck grew bigger with each step, and as I walked, the sun reflected off something in the middle of the greenery. It was a large pool of water—I was sure of it. The excitement of the scene sent a surge of energy down my legs. I ran.

The greenery changed from a blur to the recognizable shapes of palm leaves and tall grass. I ran until my feet brought me to the edge of the water, where I dropped to my knees and thrust my hands in. I threw water in my face and mouth and tossed handfuls into the air above me, where it came crashing down like rain. It felt so good that I slid in hands first, my body sliding along the bottom.

Instead of sand, the bottom surface was a hard surface of some kind. It had the granular appearance of sand, but was smooth to the touch. The entire pond floor was one solid surface, with no breaks, like a giant bowl. The peculiar nature of this pool of water should have given me great reason to investigate further, but my hunger took over, and my attention turned to the fruit hanging in the nearby trees.

As I picked and ate the fruit, I studied my surroundings, trying to decide which way to go. That's when I saw something horrible. On the horizon, a sand storm was coming my direction.

The storm was far away, but it barreled across the desert floor like water bursting from a broken dam. In a few minutes, the storm was going to sweep me away to my death. I looked around for somewhere to hide, but I remembered what the guide had told me.

"The storms are impossible to outrun and the desert provides no shelter strong enough… If you see a storm, you are already dead."

As I told myself it was time to accept my fate, the earth began to shake. It wasn't caused by the approaching storm, though—it was something beneath the sand. I realized that the shaking was limited to the area immediately around me, but a stone's toss from where I was, the sand was still. The ground shook with so much force that I lost my balance and fell to my hands and knees. The earth shaking intensified as I scrambled to the calm area.

Just as I reached safety, a massive object blasted out of the sand where I had been standing. It was round like the trunk of a tree but bigger than every tree in the oasis and covered in rough, heavy scales, like one would see on an ancient tortoise. The top of the object was flat, like a tree stump.

Almost simultaneously, a second, third, and fourth identical object blasted out of the sand—one at each corner of the pool. I retreated toward the trees as a fifth object shot out of the sand at one end of the pool. It was still covered in scales, but it was pointed at the end, instead of flat. Finally, a sixth and much larger, bulbous object emerged from the other end of the pool. The bulbous portion split open and a loud, groaning yawn echoed through the air.

In that moment, I realized that these were not separate objects but part of the same creature! Sticking out of the sand were the legs, tail, and head of something fantastic. The head lurched forward and dunked itself into the water, its massive mouth sucking up nearly all of it like a vacuum. As soon as it was done drinking, two of the legs started swinging back and forth, and the remaining water rocked and splashed with each swing. The pool floor was the creature's belly!

The creature started to turn sideways and lift itself out of the ground in a reverse scooping motion, and the remaining water spilled out and was devoured by the hot, dry sand. The legs continued to swing back and forth as the shelled body rose higher, exposing his tortoise-like body. With one final swing of its legs, the enormous creature flipped completely out of the sand and stood upright. Before me was the amazing Drobwobble tortoise.

The tortoise was wider than a house and towered over the treetops. He opened his mouth and stretched his massive neck toward one of the large palm trees, clamped down on it like a child placing a lollipop into their mouth, and then, with a powerful jerk of his neck, ripped the tree out of the ground, roots and all. He lifted his head high into the sky, then swallowed the entire tree in a single gulp. The tortoise did the same thing with each remaining tree, and in less than a minute, he had eaten everything in the oasis.

Had this creature been lying on its back and creating a water source for these plants as it hibernated in the sand? Had he sensed the approaching storm and emerged to feast on the trees before the storm whisked them away?

Now, with all the vegetation eaten, the Drobwobble tortoise took notice of me. I feared the plants had not satisfied his appetite and that he intended me to be dessert. His head swooped down until we were face to face and he breathed slow and long through his nostrils. When he exhaled, the cold air was so powerful that it pushed me backward.

As he studied me, I felt the wind pick up and grains of sand pelting my exposed skin. The tortoise and I both turned toward the horizon—I'd forgotten about the sand storm. In a matter of seconds, I would be dead.

I turned back to the Drobwobble tortoise for one last look. If I was going to die, I figured I might as well take in the magnificence of this creature one last time. When I turned, however, all I saw was the tortoise's wide mouth descending upon me. It closed around me like a dark cave, and then I felt the motion of his head lifting and moving to the side. Without warning, his mouth opened and he spat me back onto the sand.

The harsh winds of the approaching storm still rushed past me, but I no longer felt the sun burning down. I was lying beneath the Drobwobble tortoise's domed belly, which hovered over me like a giant, upside-down bowl.

Just before the wall of the storm was about to crash into me, the tortoise pulled his head, tail, and legs into his shell and the bowl-shaped shell dropped down. Everything went pitch black and silent, other than the thumping of my heart and the panting of my breath. Under the protection of the tortoise's shell, I was saved from certain death.

When the storm had passed, the Drobwobble tortoise stretched out his legs and lifted his body. I came out from under his belly and looked up.

"Thank you!" I yelled.

The tortoise nodded and let out a calming hum that rattled

the air. He then went to work using his front legs and head to dig a massive hole in the sand. When he was done, he rolled over, dropped into the hole, and pulled his legs and tail into his shell. Using his long neck, the tortoise filled in the spaces around him with sand until his outer shell was concealed.

The tortoise then began flexing his throat like a bird regurgitating food for its young. Instead of spitting out food, however, all the water the tortoise had sucked up rushed out of his mouth like a giant waterfall and filled his bowl-like belly once again with water. Next, he spat seeds from the trees he had eaten, blanketing the area around the pool.

Using his mouth, he pressed the seeds into the ground and then splashed water on top of the seeds. He gave me a final glance and then his head disappeared beneath the sand and back into his shell.

Sophia's alarm rang. It was 6:55 A.M.—time to return the book before her dad awoke.

THE START OF CHANGE

Once again, Sophia's mind nearly burst with all her questions, and she hoped returning to the zoo might prove helpful, so she vacuumed down her breakfast and headed out the door and up the zig-zag road. She squeezed through the loose board in the fence and headed straight for the Drobwobble tortoise exhibit.

It appeared just as she'd imagined, but there was no visible sign of life. Sophia narrowed her eyes and scrutinized every inch of the exhibit, but there was nothing—no movement.

For a brief moment, that awful thought that occasionally entered her mind returned. What if Mayor Monev was right? What if there was no such thing as the Drobwobble tortoise?

Sophia dropped her head and was about to walk away when she felt a sudden urge—the same type of urge that had driven her to climb the great Jumondo tree. She hopped over the short barrier surrounding the exhibit, marched to the edge of the pool, and dropped to her knees. She closed her eyes and held her right hand above the surface for a few seconds before plunging her hand in.

Her fingertips shot through the water and touched the bottom of the pool, and it was not rough or grainy like sand. She pressed her palm down and rubbed the smooth, slippery surface, just as Ferbert had described. She heard—or, rather, felt—a calming hum.

When she opened her eyes, the scene was the same, but the feeling Sophia had experienced when she found the sap-tap with her dad's initials came over her again. She smiled, and as she did so, her invisible armor softened a little more.

Just then, she heard a school bell ring in the distance. "Oh no! I'm late."

Sophia ran to school and was breathing heavily as she crept through the classroom door. Mrs. Blantly wrote on the whiteboard at the front of the classroom, so Sophia started tip-toeing to her desk. She was only a few steps away when she heard it.

"Look who decided to finally show up. Go ahead, everyone, turn around and look at the girl who thinks she's too good for school." Mrs. Blantly turned to Sophia and continued, "You might as well stop what you're doing and march your way to—"

Mrs. Blantly had been scowling, but when Sophia looked up, the teacher went speechless and tilted her head with confusion. Sophia looked around the room and saw similar looks on the faces of the other children. Their expressions had morphed from irritation to intrigue, as if they were seeing a weird-looking stranger for the first time.

"To… to… um…" Mrs. Blantly tried to continue, having forgotten what she intended to say, but it was no mystery to Sophia what her teacher was about to say. Sophia had already started turning around, knowing she was about to be sent to the principal's office, but to her surprise, Mrs. Blantly spoke two words the girl had never, ever, expected to hear from the woman, "I'm sorry."

Sophia's mouth dropped open, as if she were about to say something, but nothing came out.

"I'm sorry," Mrs. Blantly repeated, blushing. "I don't know why I took that tone with you—it was uncalled for. Please, take your seat."

Sophia moved slowly, now skeptical of the whole situation. She listened to the whispers of the children as she waited for this strange turn of events to twist into some kind of cruel joke, but it didn't.

"She looks different," she heard one of the kids

say.

"Yeah, but in a good way, I think," said another.

"It's weird," said a third student. "I almost want to be nice to her."

Sophia looked down at her clothes and gently patted her own hair and face. Her hair was the same as it always was, and the clothes she was wearing were not new. Nothing about her appearance seemed any different. As far as she could tell, she looked exactly the same as every other day. The only difference was the way she felt: good.

For a split second, she wondered if Mrs. Blantly and the other children could see how good she felt, but that seemed crazy, so she pushed the question out of her mind.

BLORTERBLUM BEAST

By the third night, Sophia was already an expert at sneaking Ferbert's book away to her room. She hid under her covers with her light and peeled back the pages to where she'd left off.

After leaving the Drobwobble Desert, I continued my journey to the Blorterblum Wilderness. I gathered a backpack of supplies, and a local merchant insisted that I take a rifle for my protection, but I refused. I spent a week marching across the land and sleeping in the trees before I came across a small Blorterblum village.

It was small with no more than twenty-five huts, and the people were delightful. They threw a feast for me the night I arrived with music, dancing, and storytelling. One of the stories was particularly intriguing to me.

The tribal elder told of a beast that lived in the wilderness just outside the village. "The beast stands twenty feet tall—nearly forty when it rises up on its hind legs," he explained in an animated voice.

I immediately asked him where I might find the beast and what it looked like, but the tribal elder just laughed. "You hunters are all the same, always wanting to know where to find this beast," he said with a big smile. "It is not a real beast—just a story we tell our children so they don't journey far from the village." He laughed. "I am sorry, but you will not be able to kill an imaginary beast on this hunting expedition."

"I am no hunter," I told the tribe elder, "and I certainly don't want to kill any creature."

"Hunter or no hunter, there is no such beast—except maybe in your mind. It is what you call a… legend. Yes, a *legend.”*

I was certain the elder was wrong, but he was an old man, and nothing I could say would change his beliefs, so I didn't say anything else. When it was time to sleep, the tribe elder offered me his hut.

“Many thanks,” I told him, “but I will sleep in one of the trees.”

“Make sure you find a tall tree,” he said with a wink. “I would hate for the beast to gobble you up in the night.” The villagers exploded with mocking laughter as they left me and went to their huts.

I found a tree just outside the village, and as I was about to climb it, I felt a gentle tug on my shirt. When I looked down, I discovered one of the village boys.

“Mister, I must speak to you,” he said in a hushed voice.

I let go of the tree and squatted to his eye level. “What about?”

The boy looked over his shoulder and then back at me before he whispered, “About the beast.”

Before I could respond, the boy threw his hands over my

mouth. "Not here," he said. "When the sun rises, walk directly into it until you come to the stone hill. I will meet you there. We will catch mice and then the beast."

"Stone hill? Mice?" I asked, but the boy was already running back to the village.

The next morning, I did just as the boy directed. About five miles outside the village was a massive stone hill spider-webbed with cracks. The boy stood next to a six-inch-wide crack, waiting. At his feet was a cage the size of a shoebox made of sticks he had lashed together.

When the boy saw me, he put his finger to his mouth, warning me to be silent, looked back to the crack and sprinkled a small amount of seed on the ground just outside it. After a minute or two, a mouse cautiously poked his nose out of the opening and sniffed around for just a moment before inching toward the seed. The boy let the mouse take a few bites before dropping his cupped hands over it.

"We should probably catch at least nine more," the boy said as he scooped the mouse into the cage.

"I'm sorry," I said. "I'm confused. What do we need the

mice for?"

"The beast," he explained, in frustration. "Isn't that why you came? He is real, you know, and he likes mice. Big beast, eats small," he said with a smile. "At least, I think he does. I've never waited around long enough to see him come out of the bushes."

"Well, then I guess we should get on with the mouse hunt," I replied. I extended my hand for a handshake to officially introduce myself. "By the way, I'm Ferbert Flembuzzle."

"I'm Nintok," he said as he stared at my hand, his confused eyebrows squashed together. After a minute, he finally spoke. "I don't know who taught you how to catch mice, but they are not going to jump into your hand." He handed me a bag of seed. "Do it my way."

Nintok was much better than me. By the time I caught my first mouse, he was scooping his ninth into the cage.

"This is good," he announced, and we proceeded into the wilderness. As we walked, Nintok told me everything he knew about the beast. "My parents always said I was a troublemaker—that I never listened and never stayed where I was supposed to—and I suppose they were right. They told me stories of the beast, but I never believed their tales and told them I wasn't afraid of anything. One day, I wandered outside the village. I suppose it was not that far, but for how young I was, it seemed very far.

"That's when I found it," Nintok explained. "I was walking through a field and tripped over a rotten log that crumbled under the weight of my leg. A hundred mice scurried out from underneath it, and although I wasn't afraid of a beast, I was afraid of mice. Can you believe that? I wanted to scream as the mice darted this way and that. They ran behind rocks, bushes, and trees and vanished in the tall grass. A dozen mice ran into a bush, like that one." Nintok pointed to a bush as tall as some of the neighboring trees as he placed the wooden cage on the ground. "And then the bush shook. When the shaking stopped, the mice did not come out—the beast was hiding inside."

"Did you see it—the beast?" I asked.

"No." Nintok dropped his head shamefully. "I was too afraid. I ran. When you came, though, I decided I wasn't going to be afraid, anymore. No more running for Nintok."

He opened the cage and sprinkled a little seed outside the door. The mice were skeptical but eventually took courage and slowly made their way toward the treat. When the seed was gone, they looked at each other and then at Nintok and me. Realizing their newfound freedom, they scurried in all directions, including toward the bush Nintok had pointed out moments earlier.

The moment the mice disappeared behind the leafy cover, the bush rustled and shook. It didn't shake much, but it was more than a mouse could do. Nintok and I grinned at each other and then inched closer. There was something familiar about the bush. It was not the way it looks. It was the way it made me feel as I stepped closer. It was the same way I had felt while sitting in the branches of the Jumondo tree and at the edge of the oasis pool in the Drobwobble Desert. It was a feeling of adventure, but my excitement was short-lived.

I reached out, but before my fingertips touched the leaves, the bush rustled again we heard a low, guttural growl. Nintok and I both turned just in time to see a massive, fully-maned lion emerge from around the back side of the bush. The lion's walk was both graceful and aggressive, and he dropped his mouth open, showing off his sharp teeth.

Nintok and I stepped backward, but each step back was matched by the lion with a step forward.

"I forgot to mention," Nintok whispered. "The lions here also like mice. Of course, I should also tell you that it usually just makes them hungry for a bigger, meatier meal, though." He looked at me with a nervous smile. "Something like us."

"I don't suppose you have any tricks for getting us out of this situation, do you?" I asked.

"Yes, there is one thing to do, but it's not really a trick."

"Okay," I said, exhaling deeply. "You just tell me what to do."

"B… B…. Before I do, I have a confession. Remember when I said there was no more running for me?"

"Sure."

"Well, change of plan." Nintok gave me a look that begged for forgiveness as he turned and sprinted away. When he got to full speed, he announced his plan: "Run!"

"Wait! What?" I called out as I stumbled over my own feet and fell to the ground.

"I'm sorry!" Nintok yelled back.

He was already so far away that I could barely make out his voice. It was clear to me what he was sorry about: the unspoken part of his plan. It was based on the age-old rule of survival that you don't have to be faster than the predator, just faster than the other prey—me.

I scrambled about until I was on my back and could see the lion standing only a few feet from me, licking his lips. I pressed myself up on all fours in a crab-walk and started scurrying backward. The lion continued to calmly and causally approach me.

"Listen, I—I don't think you're going like how I taste very much," I started pleading with the lion, as if he could understand me. "Yeah, I'm sure of it. Plus, I'm so skinny that there's hardly any meat on my bones; all the work you'll have to do to eat me will probably just make you hungrier."

The lion swaggered closer until our noses practically touched. It was clear that he enjoyed drawing the whole experience out, which I suppose was lucky for me, because I'm not sure things would have turned out the way they did otherwise.

At the very moment I had accepted that my fate was to become lion lunch, I saw movement behind the animal. I tilted my head to the side to get a better view, and the lion, curious to know what I was looking at, turned his head as well. The bush was moving again—rustling, at first, but then it rose up and shook like a wet dog.

The thousands of leaves on the enormous bush folded and wrapped around the branches to which they were attached. The branches then went limp like wet spaghetti, but with the thickness and texture of dreadlocks. Every inch of the creature was covered by this rough, coarse, shaggy fur that had once been stiff, leaf-covered branches. The peculiar fur draped over her body so the only features visible were the creature's dark eyes, flat nose, and two long teeth that protruded downward and out of her mouth.

The Blorterblum bush beast was real!

I was so caught up in the amazing scene that I almost

forgot I was supposed to be lion lunch. The lion also forgot and swung his hind legs around to face the creature before taking a deep breath and roaring.

The bush beast dropped her head close to the ground and studied the lion. She then shot upward on her hind legs, like a rearing horse, and true to the legend, the beast's head towered nearly forty feet off the ground, casting a dark shadow over the lion and me. She stood on her hind legs for a brief moment before hammering back down on all fours, a giant cloud of dust and dirt exploding from under her paws. She let out a shrill, crackling roar far louder and longer than the lion's.

The lion's eyes widened and his legs flailed about until he was turned around and running away. Once again, I found myself the slower prey. The Blorterblum bush beast, however, eyed me for a few seconds before turning and bounding deep into the wilderness.

Even though Nintok left me to be lion lunch, I returned to the village to tell him what happened. He glowed with delight and gushed with apology as I recounted every second of *what took place after he abandoned me.*

"No more running for me—I mean it this time," he said just before I took my journey to the Rumgumhum Canyon.

Sophia's alarm sounded. Fighting the urge to keep reading, she closed the book and returned it to the drawer.

As she had done the last two days, she got ready and went straight to the zoo, but this time she left a little early, so as not to be late for school again. At the entrance, she slipped through the fence opening and ran to the Blorterblum bush beast exhibit. She carefully studied the leaves and branches on the bush in the middle, imagining what it would look like if the leaves folded and the branches went limp and a shaggy creature arose. She could almost picture it.

"Come on," Sophia sighed. "Just give me a sign. Please."

As she pleaded with the bush, a mouse ran across

the exhibit and under its thick leaves. The bush rustled ever so slightly—not much, but more than a mouse could do.

It wasn't the grand scene she had hoped for, but it was something. The good feeling inside of her grew and her invisible armor softened a little more, and Sophia headed to school.

When she entered the classroom, she discovered her desk had been repositioned. It was still in the back of the classroom, but it now faced forward. She smiled at Mrs. Blantly, who gave Sophia a half-smile in return. Sophia took her seat, and for the first time all year, she was permitted to look at what Mrs. Blantly wrote on the whiteboard.

The day only got better. In each class, Sophia noticed students and teachers smiling at her and overheard quiet whispers about how nice she looked. This change made no sense to her, so she was cautious about enjoying it, always mindful that it might be the setup to an elaborate joke. However, deep down, she had a gut feeling that it was real. Somehow, someway, Ferbert's book was changing her and, in turn, changing everyone around her for the better.

RUMGUMHUM CANYON

On the fourth night, Sophia hid under her covers and read about her dad's adventures to the Rumgumhum Canyon.

The Rumgumhum Canyon is situated in the middle of the Gumhumrum Forest just beyond the Humrumgum Hills, and it is a three-day hike from the entry of the Gumhumrum Forest to the edge of the Rumgumhum Canyon.

Almost everything in the Gumhumrum Forest is poisonous to humans, including the only food that grows there: Gumhumrum berries, which are believed to be the most delicious in the world, but are also the most poisonous—at least to humans. A single bite brings death before the chewed berries reach the stomach. The animals in the forest are immune to the berries, but since their entire diet consists of them, their meat is nearly as poisonous as the berries.

Sophia couldn't help but snicker when she read about Ferbert getting stuck in the thick vegetation only two steps into his journey and being forced to leave his supplies in the clutches of vines and branches, which meant he had to live off the land. Her stomach lurched when she read about what he was forced to eat for three days straight: Gumhumrum slugs.

Gumhumrum slugs were the only nonpoisonous thing in the forest, and according to Ferbert's book, they were a putrid bug covered in slime as thick as cold honey and tasted like rotten, maggot-infested seaweed. The slugs' green innards had the consistency of sweaty gym socks covered in tar. To top it all off, the slugs made Ferbert's breath so terribly rancid that plants wilted if he exhaled too closely to them.

Sophia went back to giggling as she read about the colony of fire ants that followed him down the rope as he descended the Rumgumhum Canyon. After failed attempts to swat the attacking ants, Ferbert, in a desperate, final effort, tried to blow the ants away. Under normal circumstances, this would have been a laughable effort, but luckily he'd eaten nothing but Gumhumrum slugs for three days, and his breath was rancid. No, it was beyond rancid. It was revolting. It was unbearable… especially to the fire ants.

The ants nearest to him did an immediate about-face and started scampering back up the rope. They fled until they were outside the fog of his breath. Then, the ants turned around and marched back down the rope. Ferbert blew out his foul breath once more, and the ants fled. This pattern continued until the section of rope just above him was clean and clear, but immediately above that, was a growing, massive ball of ants that bobbed up and down the rope like a confused elevator.

The bright, red ball soon attracted a flock of hungry, squawking birds that devoured the army of ants. Unfortunately, that was not all they devoured. Sophia gasped as she read about the birds pecking through each thread of the rope until the moment Ferbert was cut loose and fell down the canyon, which was the very moment he discovered the Rumgumhum reptilian.

The Rumgumhum reptilian lived on the sheer face of the canyon wall and looked like a four-legged prehistoric dinosaur, if the dinosaur had been flattened to the thickness of pancake. Despite being an enormous creature at nearly one hundred feet long from the tip of its nose to the end of its tail, it was almost invisible to the untrained eye when it stuck to the canyon wall like a sticker. Its smooth, rock-like skin matched the canyon wall perfectly, and the only indication that the reptilian was present was that, when the rock wall warmed in the sun, the body of the Rumgumhum reptilian remained cool to the touch.

When Ferbert fell, the reptilian peeled away from the wall and cut through the air like a flying squirrel. It caught Ferbert with its gigantic lizard tongue, then curled its body until it became a parachute and gently lowered him to the bottom of the canyon.

When Sophia's alarm went off, she didn't bother waiting for her dad. After returning the book, she went straight to the kitchen and poured herself a bowl of cereal. She was slurping down the last of the milk when Ferbert came into the kitchen.

"There you are," he said. "You gave me a little scare when all I found was your empty bed this morning. It's not like you to be up before me. Did you sleep okay?"

"Um, yeah, sure," Sophia stammered. He didn't appear to expect more of an explanation, but she felt the need to cover her tracks. "I have an assignment I need to work on this morning. In fact, I will need to leave early most days to work on it before school—it's the only time I can work on it."

It wasn't a complete lie. Going to the zoo was a project of sorts, and the early morning was the only time she could sneak away. Still, it felt like a lie to Sophia, and she wished she hadn't said anything.

"Oh yeah? What kind of project?" Ferbert asked.

She was not prepared for follow-up questions. "It's a… a project about… wildlife." Again, it was only a half-lie.

"Can't wait to see it," Ferbert said. "I'm a huge fan of wildlife."

Sophia felt a tinge of guilt and worried that, if she let the conversation continue any longer, she would say something else she might regret. "I should probably get going," she finally mustered, and then she made her way straight for the zoo.

At the zoo, Sophia stood in front of the Rumgumhum reptilian exhibit. The far end of the exhibit was a smooth rock face several stories high and hundreds of feet across. From the barrier, it looked like nothing but a boring rock wall.

Sophia hopped the barrier, walked up to the wall, and pressed her hand against it; the rock face was already warm from the morning sun. She dragged her hand against the rock surface as she walked the length of the wall, and before she got far, she discovered a change. As her hand slid over a small ridge, the warm rock instantly became cool to the touch, just like Ferbert had described in the book.

She still couldn't see it, but something told her she was touching the Rumgumhum reptilian. Like each day before, her invisible armor faded away a little more and the good feeling inside became a little stronger.

During lunch that day, Sophia was so preoccupied with her thoughts she forgot about finishing her lunch before the other students. By the time she realized her mistake, it was too late. Gretchen Braunstein was already on her way to dump her leftovers on Sophia.

She closed her eyes and braced herself for the humiliation of being covered in spaghetti and meatballs, but nothing happened. Instead, she heard food plopping into a trashcan and a tray being dropped in the bin.

"I like your outfit," Sophia heard. She opened her eyes and saw Gretchen smiling at her—not a malicious smile but a real one. "It looks really cute on you."

Before she could process what had just happened, Gretchen skipped away.

FRIEND

Day after day, school life for Sophia kept getting better and better, and she felt less alone and afraid every day.

Each night, she retrieved the book from Ferbert's study and retired to her bed, where she read more and more about each of her dad's adventures.

After reading about the Rumgumhum reptilian, she learned of Ferbert's journey to the Capperskoppy Caverns, and how he got there through a different path than he had on his original journey. After the Rumgumhum reptilian parachuted him to the bottom of the canyon, Ferbert discovered there was no way for him to climb out. Instead, he jumped into the raging river at the bottom of the canyon and let it choose his next location.

He rode the river through the canyon and continued riding as it went underground, where he was eventually dumped into one of the many tunnels connected to the Capperskoppy Caverns.

Inside the cavern, Ferbert accidently awoke a swarm of vicious bats when he let his improvised torch drift a little too close. The bats chased, dive-bombed, and clawed at Ferbert until he threw his torch through the air, hitting and waking the Capperskoppy Cavern spider, a creature hanging from the cavern ceiling disguised as a stalactite.

After being hit by the torch, the stalactite spread open as it dropped from the ceiling and landed on eight legs. A sticky, crisscrossed webbing stretched between each of the legs so the standing spider created a cage-like dome as big as a house. It let out an awful shriek that confused the bats' sense of direction, making them fly into the webbing, where they became the spider's next meal. The spider crawled back onto the ceiling, leaving Ferbert to continue his journey.

The next stop in his adventures was the Verplickitty Swamps, where Ferbert swung from vines to get around. Sophia bit her lip when she read about her dad being pulled deep under the water by an alligator, where an entire congregation waited for him. She cheered inwardly as she read about Ferbert wrestling his way out of the jaws of the alligator and escaping just long enough to discover the Verplickitty bark back viper.

Instead of scales, the viper's outer skin was thick bark, and the snake stunk of rotting wood. While Ferbert was still in the water, the snake wrapped around him, starting at his feet and working its way to his head. It slithered in circles around his body until all one-hundred-and-fifty feet of the snake was wrapped around him like the rags of a mummy.

When the alligators came looking, they found only what appeared to be a dead log floating in the water.

In the Wungleswarp Jungle, Ferbert came face to face with the Wungleswarp mimic monkey, who had fur capable of changing both its texture and color, allowing it to take on the appearance of anything it touched. When Ferbert was looking the other way, the mimic monkey stole his satchel and hid it in the cavity of a nearby tree before taking on its appearance.

The monkey then swung throughout the jungle, causing Ferbert to think his satchel had come to life or had been cursed by a magic spell and was running away. He chased the satchel for an entire afternoon before discovering the truth. At first, he was grateful to have at least one adventure where his life wasn't threatened, but it took Ferbert a week of searching before he found the real satchel.

Sophia's heart skipped a beat as she read about Ferbert stumbling upon a tribe of manhunters while journeying to Swidwiggy Falls. The manhunters would chase a man just about anywhere—through valleys, up trees, down mountain sides, and into rivers. The only place they would not chase someone was over Swidwiggy Falls, but no one had ever gone over them and lived to tell about it.

The manhunters chased Ferbert for an entire day before he finally reached the edge of the falls. When he looked into the rushing waterfall, he discovered the Swidwiggy squid in the middle of it.

The tentacled creature had skin with the appearance of falling water. Amazingly, the squid swam upward, against the falling water, and maintained a position halfway up the falls, feasting on fish that went over the edge.

With a wink and a wave to the manhunters, Ferbert had jumped into the falls, where the Swidwiggy squid caught him and gently transported him to safety.

Sophia giggled when she read about her dad napping under a tree in the Pogsfurful Tropics and being woken by an adorable baby boar licking his face. She envied Ferbert as he described the piglet following him like a little mascot.

She snorted with laughter when the herd the piglet belonged to found Ferbert with the piglet at his heels. Believing he had kidnapped their piglet, the boars chased Ferbert through the Pogsfurful Tropics.

While sprinting down a dirt path, the ground opened beneath him and Ferbert fell into the opening, which promptly closed. The stampeding boars raced on as Ferbert realized he had fallen into the mouth of the Pogsfurful bullfrog. Its skin was a rough, textured, deep brown color. Twice the size of an elephant, the bullfrog had burrowed into the ground and waited until it heard and felt the movement of animals above. That's when it opened its mouth to let lunch fall in, but it got Ferbert, instead.

Luckily, the Pogsfurful bullfrog did not like the way Ferbert tasted, and after gumming the man in his mouth for a few moments, the bullfrog spat Ferbert back out, onto the dirt path.

In the Hamthudry Islands, Ferbert made the two-day climb to the top of the Hamthudry Volcano. It had been dormant for so many years that plants and vegetation grew on the interior walls of the volcano. When Ferbert reached the top, he learned the volcano was done sleeping.

The floor cracked and split and molten lava broke through and boiled to the surface as the volcano prepared to erupt. Outrunning the eruption would be impossible, so Ferbert looked for another means of escape.

Hovering above the lava was the Hamthudry humminghawk. It was as wide as a small plane but flapped its wings twice as fast as a hummingbird. The surrounding environment reflected off the hawk's sleek, mirror-like feathers in such a way that the bird was nearly invisible from every angle. The only sign the hawk was there were its flapping wings, which looked like heatwaves rising from the lava.

When Ferbert saw the hawk, he leapt down into the volcano, toward it. The Hamthudry humminghawk grabbed him with her talons and flew him to safety.

Sophia read about Ferbert's adventures to the Fremwemmy Wetlands, the Zaflupert Plains, the Tuffscrumble Tundra, the Yavali Valley, and many more places. She read about the Fremwemmy cattail crab, the Zaflupert elk, the Tuffscrumble cactus dragon, the Yavali boulder bear, and many more.

Each morning, she returned the book to its rightful place in the locked drawer. On her way to school, her first stop was always the zoo. She went to the exhibit of whatever animal she had read about the night before and was given a small hint that the creatures were there. Each time, her invisible armor faded and she felt even better than the day before.

Each day at school brought a new and wonderful change. Not only did children stop dumping food on Sophia during lunch, but they also stopped chasing her off the playground; she started playing during recess instead of hiding in the tree. In the days that followed, the gym teacher waited until Sophia was picked for a team before starting the game, and it wasn't long until she was being picked first. Teachers stopped sending her to the principal's office as well.

Sophia even saw changes in her grades. The morning after she'd read about the Hamthudry humminghawk, Mrs. Blantly had returned her math test. At the top, where she typically saw a red Z, she saw an A+ in thick, bold ink. Beneath that were the words "Awesome job!" and a smiley face.

"You were the only one to get every problem right," Mrs. Blantly smiled. "I think I should talk to Principal Winklestein about moving you to an advanced math class."

Everyone, students and teachers alike, treated Sophia with more kindness each day. Her most cherished change, however, came on the morning before her eighth birthday.

Upon entering the classroom that day, Sophia discovered her desk was gone. The spot in the back of the class where it had been every day for the whole year was now empty. She scanned the room and discovered it had been moved to the front of the classroom, where it had been on the first day of school.

Sophia inched her way to the front of the classroom and cautiously took her seat; the other students watched and smiled as she did so. When she was seated, she heard a familiar voice.

"Excuse me, can I sit here?"

Sophia looked up and saw Bailey pointing to the desk next to her. She smiled and tears of joy formed in her eyes. "Of course! I would love for you to sit by me," she replied.

"I'm so sorry for how awful I've been," Bailey said as she sat down. "I never should have treated you like that, and I don't even know why I did it. Is there any chance you will still be my friend?"

Sophia's mouth curled upward, forming the sweetest, most delighted smile. "I would like very much."

EMPTY DRAWER

That night—the night before her eighth birthday—Sophia set her alarm for midnight and tucked into bed. Instead of sleeping, however, she tossed and turned, thinking about how close to the end of her dad's book she was. There was still one more chapter left, but she had already read about every creature in the zoo and visited every exhibit. Sleep was out of the question as the mystery of what those final pages contained ate away at her, and Sophia laid awake and waited until Ferbert went to bed.

When she was sure he was asleep, she slipped out

of bed and tip-toed down the hallway to her dad's study. She retrieved the key and edged open the drawer, but she saw only an empty drawer—no book. Sophia's heart sank.

She pulled open every drawer in the desk and looked under it, under the chair, and on and behind the shelves. When she didn't find the book, she checked the locations a second time, a third, and then a fourth. The book was gone.

Sophia slumped over and let out a deep sigh. She dragged herself back to her bed, tears sliding down her cheeks. In the dark of her room, she collapsed on her bed and sobbed into her pillow.

Several minutes passed before she stopped crying and took a slow, deep breath. In the bravest voice she could muster, she told herself what to do. "No more being afraid. Ask him where the book is. Tell him you have to finish it."

She took another deep breath and then marched to her father's room. Outside his door, she stopped and listened to the sound of her own breathing. Sophia inched the door open, careful not to make any noise, slid through the doorway, and walked to the side of his bed. Ferbert's gentle snore let her know he was sleeping soundly.

She thought about turning and leaving, but she reminded herself of how important finishing the book was. It was too important to wait until morning.

Sophia stretched out her hand out to wake her dad, but just before she touched his shoulder, she saw something out of the corner of her eye. Her hand froze in place, and her heart stopped as she turned to get a better look and confirm that her eyes weren't playing tricks.

Resting on the edge of Ferbert's nightstand was a leather-bound book with worn edges and water-damaged pages. Sophia pulled her hand back, made certain her dad was still asleep, grabbed the book, and hurried back to her room.

As soon as she shut the door behind her, she flipped on her flashlight and pulled her covers over her head. She lifted the book between her hands and pulled open the pages to the last chapter.

THE GREATEST CREATURE

I don't tie my shoelaces anymore, because my greatest discovery came from not tying them. It happened the day I climbed to the top of the highest peak in the Nocarogubby Mountains.

I had traveled all around the world and seen scores of creatures no other man has seen—amazing creatures. I had one last place to go, and I had a strange feeling I was going to discover something even more spectacular than everything else I had seen. I just knew in my bones that somewhere out there was a creature so spectacular, it would change my life in a way the other creatures hadn't. I was certain I was going to find this creature in the Nocarogubby Mountains.

The beginning of my hike up the mountainside was pleasant; the trail was gentle and gradual. Soon, however, the path became uneven and steep, and after that, there was no path. The way became so steep that I had to get down on all fours, and the higher I climbed, the colder and steeper it got. The cold air brought soft snowflakes, and as I climbed farther still, the winds grew fierce and began throwing hard, jagged snow. The icy snow stuck to every part of my body, and by the time I reached the top of the tallest peak, icicles hung from my arms, face, and the tip of my nose. As I trudged through the deep snow, I felt that my legs and arms might freeze solid at any minute. I worried I might become a permanent fixture on the mountain, but I pushed on until I reached the summit.

I searched everywhere but found nothing but snow and wind. I was alone—there were no creatures atop the mountain and most definitely no spectacular creatures. I was the only living thing, but I wasn't going to stay that way if I didn't start heading down the mountain.

Confused and disappointed, I decided to give up my search, but before I began my descent, I realized my shoelaces had come undone. I would have tied them, but I was too cold and too tired to bend down, not to mention my fingers were so frozen that I could barely bend them. So, I left my laces untied.

With my very next step, I tripped on the laces and fell. My fall turned to a roll, and then I couldn't stop. I tumbled violently down the far side of the mountain, and as I bounced and flipped, snow stuck to my body and snow stuck to that snow. Before I was halfway down the mountain, I had transformed into a massive snow boulder that grew larger and larger as it raced toward the valley.

At the bottom, the snowball I had become slammed into a tree and burst. I was thrown through the air and belly-flopped into a mud bog at the edge of a stream.

I pulled my face out of the mud, still lying on my belly. When I wiped the mud from my eyes, my sight was blurry, but I could see a creature standing on the other side of the stream. She seemed to be watching me with curiosity. As my vision cleared, I realized it was not just any creature—this creature was more amazing than anything I had ever seen. She was the most beautiful, most spectacular creature. I wish I could describe her, but there are no words in existence capable of doing so.

Sophia paused. She had been to Ferbert's zoo dozens of times and had seen every exhibit. Whatever this last creature was, it was not at the zoo. *Why? Where is it now?* she wondered. Eagerly, she went back to reading.

I stayed in the valley with this creature, and she became the focus of my life. She was like a precious jewel, so that was what I called her. Jewel moved with the grace of a butterfly, and every sound she made was like a beautiful symphony. I was convinced I would never find another creature as spectacular as her, but I was wrong.

You see, during my time in the valley with Jewel, I witnessed her give birth. The baby was just as magnificent as Jewel—maybe even more spectacular—and I planned to spend my whole life in the valley. A storm and wild beasts changed all that, though.

The beasts lived in the forest surrounding the valley and never left it. They preferred the forest shadows, which is where they stayed until the storm. Late in the summer, a huge, dark cloud appeared over the eastern mountains, blotting out the sun and throwing bolts of lightning at the ground. One vicious bolt shot out of the belly of the dark cloud and crashed into a dead tree.

The tree split open in every direction, and from within it came an explosion of sparks followed by an eruption of flames. The flames danced from branch to branch and tree to tree, consuming the entire forest. When there was no more forest to hide in, the terrible beasts surged into the valley where Jewel, the baby, and I were.

I saw the hungry eyes of those beasts fixed upon us and scooped the small baby into my arms as Jewel and I fled. The beasts chased us and the storm chased the beasts.

We ran until we arrived at a small cove, where an abandoned rowboat was being tossed to and fro against the rocks. The howls of the beasts grew as I helped Jewel and the baby board. Just as I pushed the boat away from the rocks and jumped in, a dozen of the beasts came bounding into the cove, howling and barking from the rocks as we rowed away.

We had escaped the beasts, but the storm followed us into the open ocean. The dark cloud taunted us for hours and sent waves crashing into our small boat until it could take no more.

A massive wave smashed the boat into a hundred pieces, and threw Jewel, the baby, and I in different directions. That's when I learned I was the only one that knew how to swim. I had to rescue them both, but they were so far away from one another.

I swam toward the baby and grabbed her just before she sank deep into the ocean. I then made my way for Jewel, but it was too late—she was gone, swallowed by the sea.

As the storm raged on, a light appeared. It was not coming from the sky, but from deep within the ocean where Jewel sank. Without warning, an enormous, billowing creature shot out of the water; it was brilliant white and had a soft, fluffy-looking body that matched the texture of a gentle cumulus cloud. As it flew toward the storm, however, there was nothing soft, fluffy, or gentle about its movement. Propelling itself forward with the use of a cloud-like tail and steering itself with cloud-like fins, this cumulus whale punched a hole through the storm clouds. When it did, the blue sky behind shone through the opening, and the whale swam in circles, widening the hole and chasing the storm away.

In minutes, the storm was gone and the great, blue sky was empty, except for the warm sun and the cumulus whale. At first, I was excited, but then reality took over. I was in the middle of the ocean without a boat with the baby in my arms, and I was tired. I fought to stay afloat, but I started to sink.

The last thing I remember was seeing a flash of brilliant white before everything went dark. I felt something wrap around my body, like a million of the softest feathers. The water around me rushed away as I was scooped from the sea, and then I fell into a deep sleep.

I awoke to the sound of a faint cry, and when I opened my eyes, I saw the baby lying in the sand. I sat up and discovered we were on a beach. I looked in every direction, but we were alone, so I climbed to my feet, lifted the baby in my arms, and *began walking.*

A dozen steps into my journey, I noticed something unusual. Ahead of me, on the sand, was a shadow that began moving in circles. When I looked up, I saw the brilliant white cumulus whale.

I followed as it led me down a beach and through a forest to an abandoned old house in the middle of a field. Not far from the house was a tall hill with a long, zig-zag road.

I followed the cumulus whale to the top of the hill, where I discovered a vast variety of terrains. I saw cave openings, waterfalls, steep rock faces, large, sanded areas, and more. The cumulus whale waited only a few minutes before swimming off into the distance, leaving me on the top of the hill with a hundred unanswered questions.

I returned to the abandoned home, trusting answers would come in due time.

REMEMBERING

The old, abandoned house was in bad shape but not beyond repair. It had tilted walls, holes in the roof, peeling paint, and broken windows, and the inside was infested with spiders and rodents. I found tools inside and went to work.

I chased the mice and spiders out and cleaned the inside. I fixed broken windows and holes in the roof. I squared the tilted walls and repaired sinks. I replaced rotten wood and painted the walls. I worked until the house looked brand new.

One day, while planting flowers in the yard, the cumulus whale returned. It swam through the air at the top of the hill above a tree that had not been there before. I ran up the long, zig-zag road and discovered what the cumulus whale wanted me to see. Planted firmly in the ground was an enormous Jumondo tree—or at least that's what someone without a trained eye would think it was. I saw something different.

I knew right away that this was a living, breathing, giant Jumondo bird. The question was if it the same one I had seen so long ago. There was only one way to know for sure, so I climbed up the twisted trunk until I reached the first branch. When I saw it, I nearly fell out of the tree.

Stuck in the bark was a sap-tap with the initials F.F.

Unsure of why this was happening, I looked up to the cumulus whale and called out, "Why did you bring it here?" It did not answer or even acknowledge my question; instead, it turned and swam across the sky into the distance.

For the next two weeks, I was consumed with trying to understand what this giant Jumondo bird was doing outside my door. After two weeks and without any more answers, the cumulus whale returned. This time, it had brought with it a large pool of water surrounded by sand and freshly-planted trees. I ran out and crouched at the edge, and just like the oasis in the Drobwobble Desert, the bottom of this pool was smooth and solid to the touch—the Drobwobble tortoise.

I still didn't know why the cumulus whale had brought either of these creatures, but this time I did not ask. Instead, I just watched it swim away as I called out, "Thank you. Whatever the reason, thank you."

The pattern was repeated until the once-empty hilltop was filled with every amazing creature I had discovered. To me, it was a spectacular sight, but to the unbelieving and untrained eye, it looked like nothing more than rocks, bushes, plants, grass, pools of water, tumbleweeds, and an array of trees that didn't belong in this region of the world. I wanted others to see what I saw, but knowing how long it took me to have believing eyes, I wondered how long it would take others to see these wonders. More importantly, how was I going to get people to come? I pondered that question for weeks before the cumulus whale brought the answer to my doorstep.

It was late in the afternoon and I was preparing dinner when I heard a loud knock at the door. I opened the door to find a man wearing a neatly-pressed suit and a bow tie.

"Can I help you?" I asked.

The man put out his hand and introduced himself. "I'm Gus Gates of Gus's Gates, the greatest gates on the globe, and I'm here to sell you a gate."

The man told me he had been led to my door by a cloud. I looked up and discovered the cumulus whale, and that settled it. I bought a gate from Gus Gates of Gus's Gates—a gate so large I had to use ten of the tallest ladders to reach the top.

At the top of the gate, I placed a sign that read:

FLEMBUZZLE ZOO
THE MOST EXOTIC ZOO IN THE WORLD

Sophia felt a part of her brain come to life when she read about the gate and sign. It was the part of the brain that files away long-forgotten memories. Like machines turning on in an old factory, her mind went to work, restoring those memories. She remembered being there the day the sign went up.

She remembered the zoo's opening day and the line of people zig-zagging up the road. She remembered standing at his side as Ferbert posed for photographs with Mayor Monev and following her dad from exhibit to exhibit as children told their parents about seeing the amazing creatures. She remembered the confusion and surprise she had felt as parents told their children they were wrong.

Her heart sank as she remembered the mayor's rotten Flembuzzled speech. Her body shook with disgust at the memory of him pointing his long, ugly finger at her and forbidding her to enter the zoo. She remembered the confusion and pain she'd felt as Ferbert's sign crashed and splintered to pieces at the bottom of the gate.

Sophia's memory of the following weeks also came back to her. For weeks afterward, she'd begged Ferbert to let her return to the zoo. Each time, with dropped shoulders and heavy eyes, he'd told her it was forbidden. To distract her, he would suggest they climb the maple tree behind their home and read books, and Sophia soon loved both climbing trees and the books Ferbert introduced to her. She'd read nonstop, and her mind had filled with the adventures and wonders of the world. As the weeks and months passed, her mind had pushed away the memories of the zoo.

As memories flooded back to her, Sophia felt ill for all the times she'd doubted her dad. She was angry at herself for getting in Mayor Monev's limousine and listening to his lies.

Then, Sophia remembered something else— something about her eighteenth birthday. No, that wasn't quite right. It was about her eighth birthday—something Mayor Monev had said. Her eyes bulged as the exact words came back to her: "You have only until your daughter's eighth birthday to show these level-headed citizens what you claim is here. If we don't see it, I will drive you out like the filthy rat you are."

"My eighth birthday!" Sophia gasped. "That's tomorrow!"

Just as the words left her lips, her buzzing alarm informed her that she was wrong. The morning was here; her birthday was today! Today, Mayor Monev would drive her and Ferbert, along with the zoo, from Vedner, unless everyone—child and grown-up alike—believed. Maybe it wasn't too late, but first she had to return Ferbert's book.

Sophia had her usual five minutes to return the book. She jumped out of bed and made her way to his study, where she placed the book in the drawer, locked it, and hurried back to her bed. She slipped under her covers and pretended to sleep.

After waiting for a couple minutes, Sophia realized her mistake. Her eyes flew open.

"Oh no—the nightstand!" she blurted out in a panic. "It was on the nightstand!"

Sophia looked at the clock: it was already 6:58

A.M. and she only had two minutes to get the book back into her dad's room. She leapt out from under her covers and sprinted to Ferbert's study, fumbled with the hidden key, unlocked the drawer, grabbed the book, and dashed to his room.

When she got to Ferbert's door, she placed her hand on the doorknob and turned it. As she pressed the door open, however, she heard the one sound she did not want to hear: her dad's alarm clock.

THE CLOUD

As Ferbert's alarm buzzed, Sophia froze in place and peered through the small opening in the door. She could see the alarm clock on nightstand her dad's arm reaching out and silence the alarm. She watched in horror as he sat up and examined the empty nightstand—surely he noticed the absence of his book.

For months, she had betrayed his trust by lying to him about fake school projects and reading his locked-up book without permission. She couldn't even imagine how he would react. As she took her hand off the door knob and stepped back, the muscles in her fingers spasmed and released her grip on the book. It made a soft thud as it struck the floor—not loud, but loud enough. She had no doubt Ferbert heard the thud, and she stared at the book as it bounced once and rested on the floor. Sophia then turned and ran.

She ran down the hallway, past her room, past her father's study, through the living room, and out the front door. She didn't stop to change out of her pajamas, didn't put on shoes, and didn't grab her backpack. She just ran until her body wouldn't run any more, and then she slowed to a walk.

She started to think about what she had read the night before about Jewel and her baby and tried to imagine what they might look like. She imagined the cumulus whale that had rescued Ferbert and the baby from the terrible storm.

What happened to those creatures? Why aren't they in the zoo? she wondered.

While pondering these questions, Sophia discovered that the environment around her had changed. Moments earlier, the sun was shining and there was not a cloud in the sky, but now she found herself in the center of a large shadow. Her eyes lifted to see what was blocking the sun. It was a bright, fluffy, white cloud—a cumulus cloud.

Could it be?

Sophia watched with nervous excitement, and to her delight, the cloud started moving—no, swimming. Its movement was smooth and graceful, and the cloud exposed the sun again. She pinched her eyes closed and turned her gaze downward, and when she was finally able to open them again, she discovered the shadow of the cloud moving farther away. In her bare feet and pajamas, she chased after the cloud's shadow as it darted down roads, up hills, past homes, in front of businesses, and through crowded sidewalks.

As she did so, grown-ups took notice that she had

no shoes, wore pajamas, and was in a hurry, but no one noticed the shadow Sophia chased. She was so focused on following the cloud that she didn't notice the onlookers.

The cloud eventually led Sophia to her school. By this time, all the other children were playing outside, waiting for the bell to ring. As she passed through the school yard, they all stopped playing and watched. Questions spread through the field and playground.

"Why is she still wearing her pajamas?"

"Where are her shoes?"

"Where is she going?"

Sophia took no notice of any of the students, though, and followed the cloud away from the school and to the zig-zag road leading to the zoo.

After several minutes of everyone standing in dumbfounded silence, someone finally asked, "Where do you think she's going?"

"I don't know, but I'm gonna find out," Bailey

replied as she chased after Sophia, who was already out of sight.

Bailey was followed by Theodore, who was followed by Gretchen, Garrett, Samantha, Tommy, and then everyone else in their class. Children from the other classes started following, too, and by the time Bailey reached the edge of the field, every child in the school marched behind her. When the school bell rang, no one was left to hear it.

The cumulus whale led Sophia to the gate, where it stopped. It floated in the air close enough to the gate that someone at the top might be able to reach out and touch it.

Sophia smiled and, without giving another thought, grabbed the metal bars, took a deep breath, and started climbing. She reached hand over hand and foot over foot until she finally arrived at the top; the cumulus whale was now only a few feet away.

It looked like a cloud, but there was something

different about it—something fuller and heavier than a normal cloud. It didn't shift in the winds and stayed still, except for tiny movements that resembled the breathing of a sleeping elephant.

Sophia reached out with her left hand, but it was just out of reach. She stretched farther, clasping the gate with her right hand.

"Just a little more," she told herself.

She could feel her grasp on the gate slipping as she stretched outward, and soon she was hanging on by only the tip one finger. She still couldn't reach the cloud, but she refused to pull back. Sophia pressed her body forward one last time, and her finger slipped free of the gate. Her outstretched hand brushed down through the air just short of the cloud.

As she fell through the air, the wind rushed passed her face. She was falling to her death and all of her senses told her she should be terrified, but she was not.

Sophia stared up at the cloud still floating near the top of the gate. She thought about how close she was to touching it—how close she was to knowing if her dad's adventures were true. She thought about all the times he'd been an inch away from death when the creatures had saved him. She then remembered what was written at the beginning of Ferbert's book: "Don't read this unless you are capable of believing in the unbelievable."

Sophia closed her eyes, and two words floated off her lips. "I believe."

In an instant, the wind stopped rushing past her face and she felt as though she had been scooped up by a giant hand made of soft feathers. She was still descending, but at a gentler speed. With eyes still closed tight, her feet touched the ground and the feathery atmosphere disappeared. When Sophia opened her eyes, the cumulus whale was swimming off into the distance.

She was only able to relish her excitement for a

moment before she heard a commotion of children running up the zig-zag road. Bailey led the pack as they came rushing around the corner.

"Sophia, what are you doing? Are you okay?" she inquired as she caught her breath. "You look like a crazy person running around barefoot in your pajamas."

Sophia smiled at the girl and then looked in the direction the cumulus whale had gone. It was completely out of sight, but knowing it was out there gave her courage.

"There's no time," she replied. "We have to hurry or Mayor Monev is gonna kick me and my dad out of town!"

Bailey shot her a confused looked as Sophia grabbed her friend by the hand. She yanked her toward the loose board in the fence and slipped through, and the other children funneled in behind her. As the last child slipped through the gate, one more person came running around the corner—a grown man. The man gave a smile that suggested he had been waiting for this moment for a long time before he squeezed through the opening in the fence as well.

MORE REMEMBERING

Inside the zoo, Sophia ran until she was in front of the giant Jumondo bird exhibit. In the middle was the single Jumondo tree she had climbed weeks earlier. Then, the tree had seemed like an ordinary Jumondo tree, but now she was looking at it with new eyes. A giant smile took control of her mouth and her whole body lit up with excitement.

"It's magnificent," she mumbled to herself. "How did I not see it before?"

Sophia ran to the Drobwobble tortoise exhibit and then to the Blorterblum bush beast. Her excitement swelled with each stop.

"It's all true!" she exclaimed as she looked at all the children following her. "I finally see again. My dad isn't Flembuzzling anyone—it's all true. Mayor Monev is the liar."

"What are you talking about? What did Mayor Monev lie about?" Bailey begged for answers. "What was all that you said earlier about there being no time?"

Sophia's smile faded. "That's right—there is no time," she remembered. "Today is my eighth birthday; today is the last day to believe, or it will all go away."

"What will go away?"

"The zoo," she blurted out. "My dad will have to pack up the zoo and leave, and I will have to go too. Mayor Monev is going to kick us out of town unless everyone believes. I know this sounds crazy, but this zoo is the most amazing place in the world. There are fantastic creatures all around us. You've gotta believe me." The children were speechless. "Please," Sophia begged. "You have to try."

"Try what?" Bailey asked.

"To see the creatures. You've seen them before—you just have to remember."

"Seen what creatures? Before when?" Bailey replied.

Sophia grabbed the girl by the hand and pulled her back to the giant Jumondo bird exhibit. The other children followed, and when they arrived, Sophia pointed at the tree. She was about to say something, but the words died on the tip of her tongue. She saw something that terrified her. Standing on the other side of the exhibit was the man who'd followed them into the zoo. He had been watching Sophia the entire time and heard everything she said about the zoo.

Inside, her joy halted and fear paralyzed her. She didn't want to be afraid, and her brain told her not to be, but when she saw what the man was carrying, she couldn't help it. In the man's hand was a book—a tattered, leather-bound, water-damaged book.

Bailey also noticed the man. "Who is that?"

Sophia was so overcome with fear, however, that she didn't hear the question. She couldn't take her eyes off the book. Bailey reached out and shook Sophia's arm, repeating her question.

"That's Ferbert Flembuzzle," she stammered without taking her eyes off the book. "That's my dad."

"Then why do you look so afraid?"

"Because he knows what I've been doing. He knows I've been reading his book."

"Book? What Book?"

"The one in his hands."

Bailey turned to look back at Ferbert, but she barely noticed the book—she was too captivated by the expression on his face. He was smiling a smile Bailey had seen before. Like a bolt of lightning, the memories came back to her.

Four years earlier, she had stood in that exact spot with her own father. She was the small girl who'd told her dad and a crowd of people that she could see the giant Jumondo bird. It was her father who'd told the crowd his daughter was confused. She'd been the first child to speak up when Mayor Monev first accused Ferbert of Flembuzzling the whole town.

Now, four years later, the smile that Bailey saw on Ferbert's face was the same smile he'd given her the day the zoo opened. It was the smile that said, "You saw it, and these grown-ups can't take that away from you, unless you let them."

Bailey realized she had let the grown-ups take that vision from her, and as she realized this, her eyes changed back to those she had as a young girl. She no longer saw a Jumondo tree, but instead a towering, magnificent creature standing as still as a statue. As it breathed, its leaf-like feathers shook as if blown by the wind. Bailey's whole body tingled with excitement.

"I see it," she whispered. She then began jumping up and down, shaking Sophia with excitement and yelling with joy, "I see it! I see it! I saw his smile, and I remembered everything! It's fantastic!"

His smile? Sophia thought. *But I was reading his book—I lied to him. He's gotta be furious; he wouldn't be smiling.* She was so focused on the book in Ferbert's hand that she hadn't even seen his face yet. Working her glance upward, she saw his beaming smile. Her dad didn't seem mad at all; in fact, his smile almost suggested he was proud of his daughter. Immediately, her fears washed away.

The two girls were not the only ones changed by Ferbert's smile. When Bailey began jumping about with excitement, Theodore Abbott also looked in Ferbert's direction. Through his thick-lensed glasses, everything was a little blurry, but he removed his glasses and saw the smile on Ferbert's face with perfect vision. Like Bailey, this was not the first time he'd seen the man's glowing expression. He, too, had been there the day Flembuzzle Zoo opened, and it was Theodore's mother who told him there was something wrong with his eyes when he said he could see the Drobwobble tortoise.

Ferbert's smile affected Theodore the same way it affected Bailey: it renewed his eyes to those he'd had the day the zoo opened. Instantly, everything looked as it had four years earlier and Theodore remembered everything about that day. He ran to the Drobwobble tortoise exhibit and grinned as he now saw the underbelly of a massive tortoise.

The excitement was contagious, as was Ferbert's smile, and memories of the opening day flooded back into the minds of every child there. Each of them remembered and once again saw fantastic creatures everywhere they looked. Every child dashed from exhibit to exhibit, screaming with excitement and this continued until a loud, horrible crash erupted from the entrance—the sound of metal colliding with metal.

SMARTER AND WISER

Mrs. Blantly stood at the front of her classroom, waiting for students to file in. The bell rang more than five minutes earlier, but the classroom was still empty. She double-checked the time on her watch and the clock on the wall. Usually, students took their seats within two minutes, but after ten, there were still no students.

The teacher poked her head into the hallway, which was also devoid of students. She ventured outside to the playground and the fields, but again, no students. Mrs. Blantly then went to Principal

Winklestein's office and knocked on his door.

"Mr. Winklestein?" her voice was timid.

"Mrs. Blantly," he announced cheerfully, "how are you on this fine morning? Please come in."

The woman took only a couple of steps into his office. "I'm not quite sure how to say this, so I'm just going to say it." She gently cleared her throat. "All of my students are missing. In fact, I think all of the students in the school are missing."

Mr. Winklestein's expression morphed from cheerful to confused to worried as he processed the news.

At that moment, Elmer, the school janitor, popped into the office. "Sir, I'm here to take out your garb—" he stopped. "Sir, you're looking kinda pale. You alright?"

"I'm not well. All the children have gone missing—on my watch," Mr. Winklestein confessed.

"They didn't go missing, sir." Elmer smirked. "I saw them all this morning following that Flembuzzle girl up the zig-zag road. Looked like they were taking a field trip or something."

"Following who? Where?" Mr. Winklestein jumped out of his seat in a panic.

"You know, the zig-zag road that leads to the fake zoo. Like I said, I figured the kids were taking a field trip, but I don't know what else there is to see up there."

"There isn't anything else," the principal frowned.

"Well, I thought it was a little weird because if my memory is correct, Mayor Monev locked the gate. Of course, since I see that Flembuzzle girl coming down that road every day, I thought maybe the mayor decided it was okay to let people in again." Elmer's eyes darted back and forth between the hollow, jaw-dropped expressions on the faces of Mrs. Blantly and Mr. Winklestein. "But, uh, now I'm startin' to surmise that ain't the case."

"Oh no. No, no, no." The principal paced back

and forth pulling at his thinning hair. "Mayor Monev is not going to like this. He is not going to like this one bit."

"What won't I like?" came the booming voice of Max Monev as he stood in the doorway. In his hands he held the enormous key he had taken from Ferbert years earlier.

"Mayor, sir, wh-wh-what are you doing here?" the principal stammered.

"Winklestein, today is an important day that I have been waiting four years for. Today is Sophia Flembuzzle's eighth birthday. Do you remember what that means? Today is the day I finally get to rid this town of that fool, Flembuzzle, and his twerp of a daughter. Being kind to that rotten girl has been the hardest thing I've ever done. So, before heading to the zoo, I figured I would come here and give the Flembuzzle girl the public shaming I've been waiting to all year—a proper send-off." He beamed with pride as he announced his plan. "Now, what was it that I'm not going to like?"

As Principal Winklestein explained what happened, the mayor's temper boiled over.

"How did you let this happen?" Mayor Monev screamed so loud that Mr. Winklestein's desk rattled. "How does a little girl go from being the most hated child in school to a Pied Piper that leads all of the students to the one place in Vedner I forbade anyone from going?"

"I… I… I don't—"

"I don't have time to listen to your stuttering. Just tell me who you sent to get the kids back."

"Who I sent?"

"Yes, who you sent. Surely you sent someone to put an end to this madness the minute you learned of it, right?"

"I... I… just found out. I didn't have time."

Mayor Monev released a heavy breath and, through clenched teeth, continued, "Very well. I will handle this myself." He then exited the office and slammed the door behind him

Dunger was waiting in the driver's seat of the parked limousine when Mayor Monev exploded through the school's main doors. He flung open the driver's door and climbed in, shoving Dunger into the passenger seat.

"Where's the girl, sir?" Dunger asked.

"The one place she shouldn't be," Mayor Monev mumbled under his breath as he slammed his foot down on the gas.

News of the missing children and the mayor's fury spread quickly throughout Vedner, and soon the blaring sirens of fire trucks, police cars, and ambulances followed the mayor's limousine as it careened through the town. Behind them were hundreds of cars driven by parents of the missing children, as well as everyone else in town. Every person in Vedner had abandoned work and was on the way to Flembuzzle Zoo.

Mayor Monev's limousine skidded around each turn as it zig-zagged up the hill. When the gate to the zoo was straight ahead, the mayor smashed his foot down on the gas pedal.

"Sir, perhaps we should slow down," stammered Dunger as he checked to make sure his seatbelt was secure.

Mayor Monev only gave a soft, guttural laugh as the limousine barreled toward the enormous gate, and two seconds later, an awful, terrible, dreadful explosion of metal against metal rang through the air as the limousine collided with the gate. The gate stood firm while the front of the vehicle crumpled and halted. Behind the limousine, a cacophony of vehicles skidded to a halt, bumpers smashing together and horns blaring.

The entire parking lot was filled with cars squashed bumper to bumper and door to door. The cars were crammed together so tightly that doors wouldn't open. Drivers were forced to climb out their sunroofs or crawl through open windows from the cab of their car to the cab of the next car, and so on, until they reached the last car in the line.

Mayor Monev emerged from his limousine wielding the giant key and screaming, "Flembuzzle! Where are you, Flembuzzle?"

He stomped across the crumpled hood of the limousine as smoke billowed up from the engine, unlocked the gate, and kicked it open. As he did, Ferbert and the children came running around the corner.

Mayor Monev rushed at Ferbert; before the man could say anything, the mayor lifted his long, ugly finger and jammed it into Ferbert's chest.

"I'll not hear one word out of your mouth, Flembuzzle. Every parent in Vedner has been worried sick about their children, only to discover you and your no-good daughter have kidnapped them and brought them to this… this… this place." He then turned to the chief of police. "If you will please cuff Flembuzzle and take him as far away from Vedner as you can."

"Yes, sir."

As the chief pulled a pair of handcuffs from his belt and moved toward Ferbert, Sophia jumped between them. "Please don't. My dad had nothing to do with this. It was me." Sophia paused for a moment. "It's my fault—cuff me."

She lifted her hands, ready to accept the handcuffing, but the chief just looked at her and then at Mayor Monev. "I'm not gonna put cuffs on a child."

"Fine," the mayor grunted as he yanked the handcuffs out of the chief's hands. "I seem to be the only one willing to do what's necessary. Have you all forgotten this man Flembuzzled us all? Have you all forgotten today is the day of his reckoning?"

Mayor Monev started toward Sophia and Ferbert, but before he could cuff either of them, Bailey jumped in the way. "They're not Flembuzzling anyone! It's all true."

"Out of my way, girl," the mayor snapped.

"No, I'm not going anywhere. Sophia and her dad shouldn't have to go anywhere, either."

Embarrassed, Bailey's father cut through the crowd and made his way toward her. "I'm sorry, everyone; my daughter must be confused again," Mr. Cottonwood announced as he came near her. "Bailey, please don't make a scene. Just move out of the mayor's way—we grown-ups know what's best."

Instead of shrinking in embarrassment like she had years earlier, the girl stood tall. "Dad, I am not confused, and I will not move."

"Neither will I," Theodore called out as he joined Bailey, "It's all true."

The rest of the children joined Bailey and Theodore.

Mayor Monev turned to the parents. "Do you see what he has done? He's done it again, casting spells on our children! We cannot allow this, anymore. The deal was that Ferbert Flembuzzle and this imaginary zoo would be driven out of Vedner on his daughter's eighth birthday, unless we started believing his ridiculous lies. Well, today is that twerp's eighth birthday, and I still don't see any animals and neither do any of you. It's time we end this nonsense."

There was a grumbling endorsement from the parents.

Bailey stepped forward. "What about us? We believe."

The mayor exploded with rage and turned to the children, "It doesn't matter what you believe; it never did! It's time you kids realize we grown-ups are smarter than you—smart enough not to be fooled by that fool." He pointed at Ferbert.

Dunger whispered in Mayor Monev's ear, "Sir, I think you may be coming on a little too strong against the kids. You don't want to lose the parents."

The man nodded and, in a much calmer tone, continued, "What I mean to say is we grown-ups have been on this earth for much longer than you. Our years of experience and education have made us wise and mature. We know when trickery is involved, and we only want what's best for you. We only want to protect you from Flembuzzle and men like him." Mayor Monev shifted his attention once more to Ferbert, and in a much sterner voice continued, "Now, a promise is a promise. Since none of the adults believe in your imaginary animals and your daughter is now eight, it's time you left."

"Are you certain that's what you want?" Ferbert asked, disappointed. "Are you certain you want to trust your wisdom and education, rather than your children?"

"We've never been more certain about anything," Mayor Monev snapped. "Leave." The crowd echoed the command until it turned into a chant.

"Very well." Ferbert reached down and took Sophia by the hand. "It's time for us to go."

He lifted his free hand to his mouth and whistled;

the sound glided through. The grown-ups stopped chanting, and a momentary silence draped over the zoo as soft rumbles soon emerged from every part of the zoo.

LEAVING

The citizens of Vedner huddled closely together as the ground rumbled. Every grown-up was consumed by fear and unsure of what to do. Should they run? Should they hide? People seemed to be looking everywhere and nowhere all at once. Many braced themselves for more intense shaking, and parents called out and ran for their children, hoping to protect them from whatever danger might come. The children, however, were not afraid, and they looked intently toward the origin of the noise.

One pointed and called out, "Look! Over there!"

Everyone's attention was directed toward the giant Jumondo bird exhibit, where the trunk of the Jumondo tree split right up the middle and the root-covered feet lifted out of the ground. The leaf-covered wings expanded and the bird's head stretched out. Giant step after giant step, the bird walked across the zoo, towering over the people like an ostrich in a colony of ants.

Before anyone could say anything, attention shifted to the Drobwobble tortoise exhibit as four legs, a tail, and a head burst out of the sand. Everyone watched in amazement as the tortoise emerged just as he had when Ferbert discovered him in the desert.

The Blorterblum bush beast stretched out her paws and roared into the air before bounding over the railing of the exhibit.

One by one, each creature burst to life. The Rumgumhum reptilian peeled of the rock face and parachuted to the ground. The Capperskoppy spider dropped from the cavern ceiling and crept from the opening. The Verplickitty bark back viper unwound from its post in the swamp, transforming from a dead log to the longest slithering creature anyone had ever seen. Several mimic monkeys materialized from the trees in the Wungleswarp exhibit, swinging from tree to tree.

The Swidwiggy squid slid down the waterfall and lurched out of the water, pulling itself with its long tentacles. The Pogsfurful bullfrog lumbered out of its burrow and caused the earth to pound with each hop. The Hamthudry humminghawk shifted the angle of her sleek feathers so she was no longer invisible.

All the animals gathered and started migrating out of the zoo followed by the Fremwemmy cattail crab, Zaflupert elk, Tuffscrumble cactus dragon, Yavali boulder bear, and many others.

"Impossible," Mayor Monev murmured to Ferbert as he watched the scene unravel. "What kind of trickery is this? How is it done?"

"You will deny what you see with your own eyes?" Ferbert frowned in response. "Your wisdom has failed you."

"This isn't real; it's an illusion," he declared in a desperate, almost trembling voice. He stripped an axe from the hands of a nearby fireman and said, "I'll prove it."

With the axe raised high over his head, he ran toward the giant Jumondo bird. Every eye followed the mayor as he screamed like a savage warrior racing into battle.

Sophia tugged on Ferbert's hand and pleaded, "Daddy, do something. Stop him!"

Ferbert said nothing in reply; instead, he looked down at Sophia, gave her a soft smile, and then motioned with his eyebrows for her to look up.

Flying across the sky at tremendous speed was a great, whale-like cloud. As the cloud came closer, it displayed a mouth large enough to swallow a bus.

"The cumulus whale!" Sophia gasped.

A second later, it dropped down between Mayor Monev and the giant Jumondo bird. When the mayor saw the enormous mouth of the whale before him, his body went stiff as a statue and he dropped the axe. By the time it hit the ground, the cumulus whale had already rushed past the crowd and was flying up and away.

Mayor Monev was gone.

JEWEL'S BABY

For a large man, Mayor Monev left a surprisingly small void when he vanished. When the grown-ups saw the cumulus whale devour the man and realized their mistake in listening to the man, they cheered inside—but only for a brief second. They knew they had already given far too much time to the venomous babblings of Max Monev, and a brief second was the only additional time they were ever going to give the man.

Instead, everyone marveled at the great procession of creatures walking, flying, bounding, leaping, crawling, swinging, and slithering out of the zoo. Everyone, that was, except Derek Dunger. While they were mesmerized by the spectacular scene, Dunger relished that he no longer had to live in the shadow of Mayor Money. When he saw the exotic creatures come to life, he grinned slyly as his mind started formulating evil plans. He knew this was neither the time nor place to carry out those plans. He stepped into the backdrop and slipped away.

Parents held their children tightly as they watched every last creature step out of sight. When the creatures were gone, the parents turned to Ferbert, ready to apologize for not believing, but he and Sophia were gone, too. So, parents turned to their children, instead.

Bailey's father wrapped his arms around the girl. "I'm sorry. All those years ago you saw what I couldn't. I should have trusted you; I should have believed you."

Theodore Abbott's mother took his glasses from his face as she spoke, "All this time, I've been forcing you to wear these dreadful things, but it turns out I was the one who needed an eye doctor."

Every parent begged forgiveness from their children and vowed that they would never let it happen again. Every child freely forgave and wrapped their loving arms around their parents. Then, hand in hand, all returned to their homes wondering if they would ever see Sophia, Ferbert, or the exotic creatures again.

What they didn't know was that Sophia and Ferbert were sitting comfortably on the back of the cumulus whale. After it swooped down and swallowed Mayor Monev, it scooped Sophia and Ferbert on its back, where they safely flew away from Vedner.

Sophia looked back at the long line of exotic creatures following the whale until Vedner was out of sight, and then she snuggled up next to her dad as he wrapped his arms around her. "Where will we go now?" she asked.

"I don't know," Ferbert replied. "The cumulus whale knows more than I do about where these creatures need to be. Frankly, I think it also knows where we should be, so I guess we'll go wherever it takes us."

They rode quietly for a few minutes before Sophia broke the silence. "Dad, there's still something I don't understand." She hesitated.

"Is it about what you read?" he asked. She blushed and shrank a little. "It's okay," Ferbert continued. "I know you've been reading my journal and sneaking into the zoo. I've known for some time now."

"How'd you…? When'd you…?" Sophia stumbled over her words before she finally asked, "Why didn't you say anything?"

Ferbert shrugged. "I've already had my adventure finding all these wonderful creatures; I wasn't about to interrupt your adventure of discovering them." He hugged Sophia tighter. "Now, what is it that you don't understand?"

"The baby—Jewel's baby," Sophia said. "I was all over that zoo and it wasn't there. Where'd it go? What happened to it?"

Ferbert turned to his daughter with a loving smile. "You haven't figured it out yet?"

"Figured what out?"

"You were able to see all of the other creatures, but you still can't see the most magnificent one." Sophia stared at her dad with a puzzled look that begged him to explain. Ferbert reached into his satchel, pulled out a yellow tulip, and handed it to her. "Maybe this will help."

Sophia took the tulip; as she held it, her mind flashed back to the day Ferbert had first given her a tulip while sitting in the maple tree—the same day she'd asked about her mother. She remembered exactly what Ferbert had told her about how everything she wanted to know about her mother would bloom like a beautiful tulip when the time was right.

"Your mother, Juliet Flembuzzle, was and still is the most magnificent woman I have ever know—more magnificent than any creature in that zoo. She was as precious as a one-of-a-kind jewel," Ferbert winked.

Sophia's eyes widened. "You mean Jewel is Juliet? Jewel is my mom!" She lit up with excitement as Ferbert nodded, and then her eyebrows wrinkled. "That means… Jewel's baby is… me?"

"The most magnificent creature of them all," Ferbert confirmed.

Sophia threw her arms around her dad and squeezed him tight. When she finally pulled away, she sighed, "I wish we could stay—the creatures, too."

"I know," Ferbert agreed, "but I do have a strange feeling this is not the last you or these creatures will see of Vedner."

"You really think so?" she asked, but she didn't need to. Deep down, she already knew Ferbert was right.

29440704R00141

Printed in Poland
by Amazon Fulfillment
Poland Sp. z o.o., Wrocław